Alliance
Legacy War Book 3

John Walker

Copyright © 2018 John Walker

All rights reserved. No part of this publication may be reproduced, distributed, or transmitted in any form or by any means, including photocopying, recording, or other electronic or mechanical methods, without the prior written permission of the publisher, except in the case of brief quotations embodied in critical reviews and certain other noncommercial uses permitted by copyright law.

DISCLAIMER

This is a work of fiction. Names, characters, business, places, events, and incidents are either the products of the author's imagination or used in a fictitious manner. Any resemblance to actual persons, living or dead, or actual events is purely coincidental. This story contains explicit language and violence.

Blurb

A Chance for Peace

The crew of the Gnosis is set to make history again, this time for diplomacy. A message from the Pahxin has arrived, inviting humanity to a neutral space station where they might negotiate a treaty for cooperation and peace. It seems like a perfect opportunity to gain an ally against the malevolent Tol'An and the insidious Kalrawv Group.

But a dark force musters against them, one bent on disrupting this moment of peace with chaos. The joint forces of two worlds must come together to save not only themselves but also the delicate chance for lasting peace and cooperation. As the conflict intensifies, the crew of the Gnosis is confronted with a very real possibility of defeat.

Prologue

Ezria Tolva carried the Word. It had been passed on to him from the founder of the Tol'An, Calatha Dervia, a devout Pahxin who understood that the universe could not be allowed to operate without guidance. Their own government lost sight of the fact, allowing the population to live in relative freedom.

The Tol'An rose to ensure the survival of the galaxy through enforcement but they required resources, people and the technology to hold others in check. Such a calling had struck many of their people but not all understood the divine directive. None had the vision to see how uncertain the future remained in the hands of those who allowed free will to reign.

Opposition remained strong. The Tol'An found themselves pushing against many obstacles, some of which seemed to have no plans to bend. Ezria took their resistance as a challenge, an opportunity to prove the righteousness of their cause. Nothing worth having came easy and he believed it wholeheartedly.

"Your Holiness." One of his people broke his reverie and he opened his eyes. He sat in his meditation chamber. Smooth metal walls were unadorned and there were no distractions other than the altar erected in the center of the room. A simple red cloth sat folded upon the surface but it represented the only color.

Ezria himself wore simple white robes. He kept his head shaved and his lean body fit. His was as perfect a Pahxin specimen as there could be and he worked hard to maintain himself. Pure food, no toxins and discipline kept him in peak condition. None of his subordinates would ever believe themselves to be better than their master.

He peered at the soldier through startling blue eyes, taking him in as if he were little more than a hallucination. The man shifted uncomfortably in his black uniform, his holsters emptied by the guards at the door. No one was allowed to carry weapons into the meditation chamber and he had been searched before being allowed to enter.

"Speak." Ezria spoke above a whisper but the room seemed to amplify the softness of his voice.

"I come with news of our venture on Delinare. We brought back three artifacts but the one we were sent for did not seem to be present." He shifted from foot to foot, his face contorted in anxiety. "Our scientist stated that it may have been destroyed in a landslide some time ago. We spent two days scanning for it to no avail."

"I see." Ezria sighed before approaching the man. "And you are certain you have done everything in your power to find the device? You have left no stone unturned?"

"Yes, your holiness. I am confident."

"Very well." Ezria lifted the cloth from the altar and pressed his face against it. When he pulled it away, the soldier remained before him. "Is there something else?"

"Yes, your holiness ... I'm afraid ... Well ..."

"I do not have time for stammering."

"Forgive me." The man found some courage and spoke firmly. "We lost one of our starships. It was destroyed while trying to take off. Six men died aboard. We recovered two of the artifacts they were carrying but one was completely obliterated."

"So we not only failed to procure the one item I sent you for," Ezria began, "but you also lost one of the three which was meant to placate me. Along with equipment and resources. Do you have any other part of the failure you would like to impart? Or has this poor adventure been fully described?"

"That is all, your holiness."

"Gizan," Ezria called. "Enter."

The soldier gasped, his eyes widening as a black cloaked figure entered the room. His long strides carried him to the center and he took a knee, bowing his head before Ezria. "Yes, Master?"

"Stand." Ezria gestured to the soldier. "This man has failed in his duties. Will you please assist him in understanding the error of his ways?"

"Your holiness!" The soldier stepped forward. "Please! I can make amends. Allow me another chance, to bring another crew to the planet. We will finish the scans—"

Ezria held up his hand and the man stopped speaking. "Finish? You made it clear you had done everything in your power to find the item before you left. Now you use the word finish. So you compound your incompetence with lying, is that it? Do I seem so naïve ... so foolish that you can come to me with falsehood?"

"A slip of the tongue, your holiness ..." The soldier seemed to be losing his conviction. Gizan turned his hooded head to Ezria who nodded once. A hiss of a blade leaving a leather scabbard echoed in the room and before the soldier could even stiffen, a red line appeared across his throat.

Blood spilled from the wound and the man clawed at it as he choked out the last few moments of his life. Collapsing to the ground, Ezria stepped back to avoid the pool of gore forming around the head. Executing one of their own did not please him but he could not allow his subordinates to lie without consequences.

"Thank you, Gizan. Make arrangements to get rid of ... that." Ezria refused to look at the body. "Return when you have finished."

Gizan complied without a word, dragging the soldier out by one of his feet. Two men entered and mopped up the blood, cleaning the floor with a disinfectant before retreating. When the assassin returned, he stood quietly, waiting to be addressed. The man proved loyal without question, never giving Ezria any doubt as to his integrity.

Rumor suggested Gizan worked for Calatha when they first founded the Tol'An. Some suggested they were lovers but Ezria doubted it. When Calatha passed away, he turned over the mantel through a hand written will and it did not contain any words about the assassin other than to say he should be treated with the utmost respect.

"I have received word from our spies in the Pahxin government." Ezria always spoke directly with Gizan. They exchanged no pleasantries when starting a conversation, preferring to get straight to the point. "It appears the filthy Earthlings have communicated with them. Doctor Thayne Rindala helped them."

"The traitor," Gizan said. It didn't matter to the assassin that the Tol'An had kidnapped Thayne, only that he did not perform the duties prescribed to him by Ezria. "He escaped when we attempted to take the Trindisha … If I'd been there, I would've silenced his tongue before he could reveal any more to those wretches."

"Undoubtedly," Ezria replied, "however, we have to contend with the consequences of his involvement with the Earthlings. Our people have invited them to the Golanthit Station for a parlay. It seems likely they will accept this and attempt to form a partnership with one another. I want you to take our forces and ... interrupt this gathering."

"Am I to kill them all then?" Gizan asked. There was no hint of concern over such an order. Merely a desire for information. If Ezria had asked the man to go to their home world and murder the Grand Councilor, he would have attempted it and possibly succeeded.

"No, I'm afraid we need to do something more dangerous. I want you to bring the dignitaries to me. They will make excellent examples when we do execute them but prior to their ends, I believe we can extract information." Ezria smiled. "They should be more than open to speak when we put the questions to them in a direct manner."

Gizan bowed his head. "As you say."

"Select your men carefully, Gizan ... Do not fail me." Ezria threw the last bit in every time, though the man had always been able to deliver. They'd made it something of a game.

"I will not." Gizan pressed his left fist against his chest. "Do you require anything else, master?"

"No, be quick about your preparations and let me know before you depart. I believe you will want to be in the area before they arrive and know you will face their military. Do not hold back on those fiends. Destroy whatever ships you must and kill anyone in your way. There should be no mercy for those who would deny our dominion."

"Your will be done." Gizan spun on his heel and departed, leaving Ezria to consider the upcoming mission in private. With his best assassin on the job, there was no doubt he would have the ambassadors in his grasp. What he would do with them needed some planning. Simply killing them might not get his point across but starting a war between two cultures …

The Pahxin would annihilate those filthy rats. I still cannot believe they have two of the Trindishas. I would rather my own people reclaim them than to allow primitives access to such power. Before this month is done, I intend to see their world burn and their people suffer. Then we can return to attaining dominion over the galaxy … so we might save it from the threat.

☐

Chapter 1

Captain Desmond Bradford yawned, rubbing his eyes with the heels of his hands. The clock beside his head buzzed moments before, letting him know they would be emerging from hyperspace in ninety minutes. This gave him plenty of time to get cleaned up, grab a meal and head to the bridge before they arrived home.

Reports on his computer kept him company through his normal routine though they weren't exciting. Systems showed green with minor issues here and there throughout the ship. Medical stated they had released all injured personnel back to their quarters. The biggest problem came from their damaged fighters, which required dry dock to complete repairs.

Agent Cassie Alexander provided him with an update on the research they were performing on the data they discovered during their last mission. She and the two Pahxin doctors had categorized it and it was organized in an easy to digest manner for their peers back on Earth.

When they arrived, they'd be able to dive in and extract even more than the crew had during the short time they had had to study it.

Desmond wondered about the agent and worried about whether she was taking care of herself or not. Every time they went into hyperspace, she seemed to work through the trip and when they arrived, she was bright eyed and ready to go on the bridge or in the tech labs, depending on what they required.

Frankly, the woman seemed to be full of boundless energy. Still, it had benefited the ship greatly and he wasn't going to complain. She even went on the away mission to the space station and received positive feedback from the marines who went with her. *I guess the woman knows what she's doing.*

As captain of the vessel, he needed to worry about everyone on board though. If anyone pushed themselves too far, they might not be at their best when the chips were down. He decided to have a talk with her when they returned and ensure she was taking proper reset times at the very least.

The two doctors, on the other hand, he was confused by. Desmond didn't know what those men required to keep going. Food, sleep, all the human necessities may have been very different, despite the physiological similarities between them. Reports suggested they retired to their rooms once in a while but like Cassie, they seemed tireless in their pursuit of knowledge.

"Captain," Commander Vincent Bowman's voice crackled on the speaker. "We'll be emerging from hyperspace inside of thirty minutes."

"Thank you," Desmond replied. "I'll be right up."

He grabbed his tablet and left his quarters, heading for the elevator. People hurried through the hallways, passing him by with quick nods. Everyone wanted to get to their post before they had to emerge because it might be bumpy. Strapping in was advised if possible and, as if on queue, Lieutenant Salina Gold made the announcement.

"All hands, we will be emerging in thirty minutes. Please secure all cargo and belongings and report your department's status. Thank you."

Desmond disembarked the elevator onto the bridge and joined Vincent. "Anything to report?"

"No, sir," Vincent replied. "We're looking good all around. I checked the coordinates with Zach and we should be roughly three hours out from home when we arrive. Not too bad."

"Good. I'm eager to give them the data and see what they have to say. Gil and Thayne seem pretty convinced their government will be keen to talk when they see what we've learned. Allies will be nice. We've been in short supply of good will since we left home."

"I'm not sure what kind of welcome we thought we were going to get when they introduced themselves guns first," Vincent said. "Then again, how many times did humanity treat each other with similar disregard? Our history is full of times we were jerks. All the reparations in the world can't fix some of the stupid we got up to."

"Good point." Desmond turned to Salina. "Did you ever have a chance to look over the stuff we found?"

Salina nodded. "It was fascinating. They were such an advanced culture but whatever happened to them started with their star. I found some scientific reports suggesting they were attacked. Whatever went after them wanted to cause havoc with them then altered their distress signal to hurt their allies as well."

"But they didn't have any idea why?" Desmond frowned. "Seems ... strange."

"I'm speculating," Salina said, "but there's a chance they encountered a race of beings who simply did not want them there. Not to be too morbid, but they might've considered them an infestation and tried to exterminate them. As advanced as they were, they could travel to nearby solar systems. That might've represented a threat to whoever attacked them."

"Everything we gathered looked pretty peaceful to me," Desmond replied. "Though to be fair, I haven't read it all ... nor would a culture necessarily talk about being warlike I guess. Though I'm probably stretching all things considered. Anyway, if your theory is right, then I wonder why they didn't come to Earth afterward and trash us."

Vincent jumped in, "Maybe they only worried about cultures with technology capable of disturbing them. They hit the core world then allowed the signal to branch out to other places that might be a problem. I'm guessing some of the worlds that died from their attack weren't even close to ready so they acted preemptively in those cases."

Desmond nodded. "If they didn't attack them, I'm guessing the other planets would've risen up and tried to take them on. That's exactly what they seemed to be trying to avoid." He hummed. "It's a travesty that they thought the only way to contend with their perceived problem was the obliteration of so many lives."

Salina cleared her throat.

"What is it?" Desmond asked.

"Just that when the intelligence of a species dramatically overshadows that of another, they tend to lose sight of the value of their lives. Take pests, for instance. We don't hesitate to call someone out to exterminate thousands of them. Even the ones which aren't necessarily harmful, like ants. An entire colony of them can be wiped out over inconvenience."

Vincent rubbed his eyes. "Yeah, Salina. You definitely have perspective."

"It's what you need to consider when we're talking about this sort of thing." Salina shrugged. "Consider this. If we are dealing with something with such a magnitude of difference from us, then we need to be incredibly cautious in how we go about addressing them. If we encounter them at all, they may not be prone to talk."

"No one else has been," Zach muttered.

"I think we'll be ready," Desmond said. "We have plenty of warning, lots of information and the resources of a planet working on it. Couple that with some potential allies and we've got a good shot at handling whatever comes our way. However, we have two immediate threats to worry about. The Kalrawv Group and the Tol'An."

"The former bothers me." Vincent scowled as he spoke. "The believers make sense but guys out for money at all costs? Even their lives? What the heck?"

"Oh, I spoke to Thayne more about them," Salina said. "Apparently, when people join their organization, they're all in. They commit their families

"I'm sure we'll at least get that courtesy," Desmond replied. "Put a meeting together in the briefing room. Put Cassie and Salina on it but leave the Pahxin doctors out for now. If we need them, we'll know where they are."

"The data's compiled for high-level consumption," Salina said. "We're ready to present, even right now."

Desmond considered his computer screen for a moment before responding. "That's good but get down and talk to Cassie anyway. I want to ensure we've covered everything adequately. You guys know there'll be a lot of questions and we need to be able to answer them. We've had plenty of time to read through what we found."

Salina stood. "If he brought Doctor Harper, we'll be in for a real grilling. I feel like we should send the data over to them right away."

Desmond shook his head. "No, it's not secure enough and considering all the civilian satellites we have to deal with, lord knows what they've drummed up to capture that kind of data. If some amateur got a hold of it, we could create a level of mass hysteria not seen since the Black Death."

"That seems a little dramatic," Vincent said. "Surely, they know we've been gallivanting around to other systems ... visiting alien worlds. They can't possibly think we've just been prospecting dead rocks."

"They might not know the Gnosis even left the system," Desmond replied. "Depending on how twitchy the military has been. Of course, one of our own people might've leaked it on shore leave but I kind of doubt it. Our missions may well be a total secret until we have great news to share."

"You know how it goes," Zach jumped in. "We play everything close to the chest until there's something to celebrate. Then, providing it paints us in the best possible light, we tell the entire world. Everyone gets to find out how amazing we are and how our actions will benefit them. The only time it happens the other way is if a reporter gets the story first."

Desmond smirked. "Eloquently stated, Zach and accurate. Alright, folks. Get to work and inform the ship we have a VIP coming aboard. I don't mean to stand on ceremony but the admiral hasn't visited us before. Let's make a good impression."

***

Cassie ran into Vincent on her way to the briefing room. They had roughly twenty minutes before the admiral would show up. His shuttle already docked in the hangar and his escort was on the way. Desmond met them down there so that left the others to prepare the room and ensure they had everything they needed.

"How's it going?" Vincent asked. "You ready for this?"

"I suppose," Cassie replied, looking at his face for a long moment. "You're nervous."

"The fact that the admiral flew all the way out here doesn't bode well." Vincent shrugged. "I expected to see him on Earth, you know? I have a bad feeling something tragic has happened … Like, maybe bad news from the Pahxin or even another attack. Though Salina told me she ran a scan of home and everything seems fine …"

"This job has taught me a valuable lesson," Cassie replied. "Don't assume facts. Dread leads to anxiety and no one has time for it. We end up doing our jobs badly at that point because we're too caught up worrying about what might be. Imagination might be our greatest gift but it can also be our undoing."

"I admire your calm." Vincent smiled, clearly trying to shake off his gloom. "Oh well, I'll try to take a page from your book in this case. How much are we going to be able to tell him?"

"Everything." Cassie tapped the panel by the briefing room door and they entered. A crewman was putting out pitchers of water and glasses along with some fruit. Her stomach growled at the thought and she realized she hadn't made it to lunch. This is going to be exciting. Taking a seat, she tapped into the main screen. "We've got the whole briefing prepared."

"I brought the resource allocation report." Vincent gestured to his tablet. "Along with the various briefings from the folks who conducted the away missions. Did you see the biological readouts from those mutated people? I'm not an expert on anatomy but whatever happened to them really brought about some serious physical enhancements."

"Yeah, at the expense of self-preservation, compassion, mercy and diplomacy." Cassie tapped at her screen and brought her presentation up. "That place is forbidden for a reason. Maybe someday they'll rise above all that and evolve but it'll take quite a while. If they don't kill each other in the process."

"Or the planet dies completely," Salina said from the door. "Those storms will likely get worse and start hitting even the currently safe parts of the continents. I know they live underground, but their food sources will likely die out. I believe we saw the end of a species, not the beginning of a new one."

"Cheery, as always," Vincent replied. "Welcome to the party, Salina. Glad to have you."

"Thank you, Commander." Salina took a seat. "I hope that the admiral has brought good news. I'm choosing to believe he's here because he simply couldn't wait to tell us something positive."

"That's a stretch," Vincent said. "But I'll go with it. Better than the pessimism I was indulging."

Cassie chuckled. "Regardless of why he's here, we have a lot to go over. If he allows us to hit it all … this is pretty in the weeds. I tried to make the first part high-level but who knows if it's high enough? I can tell you this. The AIA is going to want the deep dive we did with Gil and Thayne. There's a lot of meat in those details."

"Indeed." Salina squinted at the screen, reading the first slide. "I'm still comfortable with it but the real people we need to sell this to are the Pahxin. They need to know what the Tol'An fears. It may well change the way they deal with those criminals. Perhaps they'll try to parlay and work together … get them to stand down and rejoin society properly."

"Unlikely," Cassie said. "I spoke with Thayne about how they were acting and I can tell you, they're far too fanatical to take orders … or give up for that matter."

The door opened and the three stood up. Desmond entered first followed by Admiral Reach and Doctor Harper. The escorts remained outside, turning to face away as the door slid shut. "Take your seats," Reach said. "I don't think we need to stand on ceremony with this type of briefing. We have a lot to discuss and I didn't want to wait for you to get back to Earth."

Desmond continued, "The Pahxin have replied to our initial communication and the admiral can tell us what was said."

"Excellent." Cassie exchanged glances with the others before going on. "I trust it was good news?"

"Somewhat," Reach replied. "Please, let's start with your mission before I get into the message we received. I'm sure you all had quite the adventure. Multiple solar systems, the neutral space station ... Do tell."

Desmond began the debriefing by explaining what happened on the space station when they went to pick up Doctor Gil Vaedra. This brought up the Kalrawv Group and what they represented, along with the details they'd picked up from their two Pahxin guests. The corporate mercenaries had plenty of data but they were technically the least of Earth's worries.

Next, they spoke about the planet they visited and described the mutants well as the strange weather patterns. The loss of their marine and the near destruction of their shuttle came up as well as the procurement of the first breadcrumb of data. It led them to an adjacent system which, for all intents and purposes, was totally void of life.

Cassie and Salina took turns explaining the data they found and what it meant before handing the reins back to Desmond to talk about the conflict and the toll it took on their men and equipment. The admiral looked grave during that part, frowning throughout the description of how far the Kalrawv Group was willing to go.

"You guys saw quite a lot of action out there," Reach said. "One thing Doctor Harper's folks have been working on is long range communications. The ability to talk to you when you're so far from home. Our research suggests that it was possible, a long time ago but how they did it ... We're still stuck."

Harper stepped in, "Yes, we've found plenty of references and some obvious cases where such technology was used but applying it to our current technology ... Let's just say we're having to do some rethinking of how we broadcast signals.

"As you know, with few exceptions, we've simply improved existing concepts with what we've learned. We may have gone as far as we can with communications."

Reach nodded in agreement. "When we received word from the Pahxin, they commented about how surprising our method was. And we thought it was pretty genius the fact we got it there so quickly. The FTL concepts we applied, with Doctor Rindala's help, made us think we were on the right track.

"Anyway, that's neither here nor there. We are working on a way to support you better in the field and that includes fast tracking another ship. It's almost done. They're on to the test phase of the various systems. Hyperspace will come last, but we'll hopefully have it fully operational inside of a month."

"That's quite a while," Desmond said. "And I doubt we have the luxury of waiting."

"You don't." Reach sighed. "In fact, we're going to be sending you back out sooner than you think … and I'll be coming with you. I believe it's time I tell you about our chat with the Pahxin. It may soon finally be time to announce to the world everything you've accomplished and seen but we're not quite there yet."

***

Desmond stiffened at the idea of taking the admiral out of the system. As a flag officer, and one of the highest value individuals in the current space program, he seemed like someone they could not afford to risk. While they had certainly proven the hyperspace drive worked safely, there were other risks involved in long distance travel.

High command either trusted the technology more than Desmond would imagine or they were simply that desperate to ensure their next mission had high-level representation. Whatever he had to tell them must've been intense because he paused again and had already built a considerable amount of drama around the announcement.

"The Pahxin communication came a day ago," Reach said. "They were intrigued by our actions so far and want to speak. We have coordinates to a mostly neutral location, a space station where we can talk. The species that runs it is like a galactic version of

Switzerland and will provide us accommodations in a non-biased environment."

"So we're doing an ambassadorial run?" Vincent asked.

Reach turned to him, "Do you have a problem with that, Commander?"

Vincent shook his head. "Not at all, sir. I'm just surprised they were ready to meet so soon."

"Our communications were too slow," Harper said. "That's why we really started to analyze our efforts. If we'd mastered real time or, at least close to real time, conversation then clearly we would've negotiated from afar. As it stands, they recommended the coordinates and we agreed to meet them there at what amounts to the beginning of next week."

Desmond hummed. "So we have time to resupply, repair our ships and take some downtime before heading back out. What're the chances of hostility?"

"Small," Reach replied. "Though I don't necessarily trust your Pahxin passengers just now … not enough to have them in this talk at least. Especially the new one you picked up. From what I understand, he operates outside their laws?"

"He's an adventurer," Desmond explained, "but I don't think he's a bad person. Still, they might want words with him. He visited one of their 'forbidden' planets and I understand why it has such a designation.

The place was outright hostile, in every way possible. The Kalrawv Group figured it out pretty fast."

"We won't turn him over or anything," Reach said. "But I want to make sure we get off on the right foot first. They can come along to the meeting. In fact, Thayne has been specifically invited but we'll keep this other guy in reserve. If there is any hostility, we're going to want to leave in a hurry ... Though if the Pahxin start it, I'm not sure what we're going to do."

"Because they can just follow us," Vincent added. "And then Earth would be in trouble."

"Let's keep it very real here." Reach leaned forward, hands clasped on the table. "If the Pahxin wanted to, they could come to our planet and kill every form of life we know. They could take the two Orbs tomorrow and there's not a damn thing we could do to stop them. The Tol'An, while dangerous, do not command their resources."

"They can raid," Desmond said, "but not commit to a prolonged assault. In other words, this bid for peace has to work or we're in a lot of trouble."

"The best-case scenario is a partnership." Reach paused, letting out a deep breath before continuing. "But if they simply don't want anything to do with us, that's better than the worst that can happen. How long before the Gnosis is ready to leave again?"

"A couple of days depending on the priority of our resources," Desmond replied. "I also need some crew replacements. Another marine lieutenant would be nice. And we've got a couple commendations to hand out as well. All this can be done at the same time as cleaning things up and getting our systems back online."

"Very well." Reach nodded. "I'm going to get out of your hair and back to the Tribute. We'll reconvene on Earth. Science teams will stick to their work with the data you've recovered and engineering will prep the ship for departure. I'd like to be ready for the jump no later than Sunday. Is that reasonable?"

"Absolutely," Desmond said. "We'll aim for a little sooner."

"Fantastic." Reach stood up and everyone followed suit. "Doctor Harper, would you like to remain on board and get a jump start on studying the information?"

Harper nodded. "Absolutely. I'd like to get some time with the Pahxin doctors as well."

"It's all yours." Reach turned to Desmond. "I'll show myself out, and thank you for this impromptu meeting. I'm confident in this meeting and your crew. Great work so far, Captain. To you and yours. See you all soon."

☐
Chapter 2

Gizan's plan required some preparation and resources but the time crunch meant improvising. He could not pull their forces from the various assignments throughout the galaxy but he had an alternative. One of their largest ships was available and he needed it to carry fighters. The Pahxin were always quick to launch one-man vessels.

Besides that, he needed distractions, destroyers or scouts at the very least. Furthermore, he could not exhaust the defenses of the Tol'An base if the enemy happened to find them. No, he needed something unexpected that would work as a means to deal with the Pahxin and their new human pets.

This meant using his swift assault vessel to acquire the extra assistance. Gizan had no lack of manpower but places to put them … That was the challenge. He ordered the battleship and its destroyer escort to an adjacent system of the Gaelirans where he'd rendezvous with them later.

A transport vessel was loaded up with enough men to crew an additional two vessels. They were ordered to give Gizan six hours before following him to his destination: a small shipyard on the edge of Pahxin space. They'd picked the location for its proximity to a resource rich asteroid field.

It was an isolated system, well away from any civilized space. Gizan's plan involved jamming their communications and commandeering two more ships.

They would have to attack the station, disable the defensive ships then claim their prizes and get out. Reinforcements would be on their way as soon as contact was confirmed as lost.

This meant they would have less than a full day to pull off the operation and be on their way. It had the added benefit of being a rehearsal for their true purpose, a chance to try some strategies before they needed to implement them. He hand-picked ten of his finest fighters to board his assault craft to make the situation happen.

Precise calculations would put them at the facility within ten hours. The transport ship would arrive a few hours later and they needed to be prepared to receive them. A misstep or any failure would lead to many deaths. Gizan was willing to take the risk, mostly because he was convinced the Pahxin resistance would be minimal.

The station defenses were flawed for a variety of reasons. One, the Pahxin seemed to use the post as a punishment for those who did not follow the rules. They didn't believe anyone would bother attacking it or they would have invested more in keeping it safe. Their Council of Defense didn't consider the Tol'An a true threat nor had they declared war on the group.

Perhaps when we take their ships and abduct their ambassador, they will begin to take us seriously. The thought made Gizan smile. He wanted the Pahxin government to show the proper fear and respect for his master. Direct action would be the only way to bring such things about. The more we kill, the more they must take notice.

The worth of the Tol'An would certainly be measured again when they concluded their mission at the Gaeliran space station. But first, they must finish their raid.

They emerged from hyperspace and took stock of the situation. Two defensive ships, one a scout and the other a destroyer, patrolled some distance from the station. Six other vessels in various states of repair and construction, were docked about the facility. A quick scan indicated they were looking at just over one hundred workers and security.

Gizan gave the order for them to begin jamming the station's communications. "Now that they are muted, charge the facility. Work on the door the moment we are in range. This will need to be quick." He gestured to three of the men. "Do not forget to sound off on the timer for bombs."

"By your will," they said in unison, nodding their heads.

"They are hailing us, my lord." The pilot announced the message without taking his eyes off the screen.

"Let them quiver in our silence. This is the most excitement these fools have had in months. Their last moments of life shall be invigorating as never before." He turned to the others. "Remember to show no mercy. You will kill anything you encounter along the way. We are not to take any prisoners either."

The message was unnecessary. This group of soldiers had worked with Gizan several times in the past and they understood his methods. Only when the grand master of the Tol'An gave orders to capture did Gizan allow a target to live. Efficiency meant cleaning every mess and that included anyone who might relate exactly what happened.

They will have to piece this story together from the destruction we leave behind and the appearance of their vessels at a different location. I may not be able to kill all the Gaelirans but they will be hard pressed to convey much about what we did.

Jamming only the station allowed them a little time before the two ships decided to investigate. First, they'd blame some sort of malfunction. Then, some kind of interference would be considered. Finally, they would head back to see what happened. If the Tol'An didn't take the control center before that time, the mission would be jeopardized.

"The doors are unlocked," the computer expert in the back announced. "I've unlocked several others as well so it should confuse them as to which we plan to enter through."

"Wise decision." Gizan appreciated the initiative, the fact that the man did what was right without being told. None of them carried names in his mind. They were simply titled after the tasks they were expected to perform. Getting personal didn't help anyone. Pretending they had value as beings beyond the tasks they were assigned served no purpose.

"How long to dock?" Gizan asked.

"Two minutes," the pilot replied. "Once we draw close, our magnetics will secure us but it will be bumpy. I recommend everyone strap in until we're secured."

"We don't have the luxury of that," Gizan said. "Hang on tight, ready your weapons and when the door opens, be prepared to shoot. I trust you've got an override on the airlock?"

"Yes, sir. We'll open both simultaneously."

Such a thing broke the protocol of every station in the galaxy save some of the seedy pirate ones. Gizan had seen it come in handy several times. They ejected entire groups through such tactics. Breaking the security to do such a thing proved particularly difficult but the Tol'An went out of their way to devise ways around such defenses.

The station was close enough to make out the individual windows but as they drew near, the ship spun to the side. The pilot allowed the momentum of the craft to carry them closer to their chosen door and when he hit the thrusters, they were jostled by a sudden tremble.

They collided with their target hard enough to cause the entire ship to shake wildly.

Something hissed and the pilot nodded. "We're lined up with the door and the magnetics have sealed! You are good to advance!"

The men held their weapons at the ready and Gizan tapped the button to open both doors. His people fired the second they had clear shots and one of them took a blow to the face from a returned shot. Screams erupted outside, men and women crying out in shock at the violence they were subjected to.

"Advance!" Gizan growled. "Move out into the hall or we will be pinned in!"

His people charged out, firing wildly. Gizan followed, taking his time for more precision shots. He counted six live targets and they were already falling back. Bodies littered the ground, the first responders who attempted to repel them. Others would be coming, the ones assigned to the doors the Tol'An didn't go through.

We must finish these quickly. The defenders were in full-on panic and their shooting suffered. They continued to miss while his own people tore them apart, killing each. The last two dropped to their knees and raised their hands, shouting out their surrender. Gizan waited to see how his people would react.

His troops surrounded them, drew their blades and cut them down. Blood sprayed on the deck as the corpses dropped to their sides, twitching out the final moments of their lives. Good, they have taken my directive to heart.

"Break up," Gizan said. "We have much to destroy and plenty of these fiends to kill. Keep your com channels open. Our coordination is key to success. Go. Be the blades of the Tol'An!"

They parted with Gizan leading four toward the control center. Once they were there, they would have unfettered access to the security systems. The slack nature of their opponents meant they were slow to initiate any sort of realistic defense. An alarm blared overhead but it didn't accompany the expected resistance.

Summoning the elevator, Gizan turned to look back down the hall toward their ship. Their pilot would defend the vessel at all costs, waiting for their return. Chances were good no one would bother to attack it. Those in the station needed to focus on the invading force rampaging through the various departments.

The doors opened and an unarmed man in a fancy suit stared at them with wide eyes. Gizan lashed up, jabbing his throat with the tips of his fingers. The victim grabbed at his neck just a moment before one of the other soldiers shot him in the hot. They tossed the body into the hallway before boarding it and heading up.

Gizan's com crackled in his ear and one of his men reported in. "We've encountered the enemy on our way to the engineering section. Six in total. We are engaging."

"Let me know when you have arrived at the reactor." Gizan had no doubt his people would win the engagement. He didn't feel a need to remind them not to fail. Their zeal would carry them through and as he listened to screams in his earbud, he couldn't help but smile at the carnage wrought by his crew.

When the elevator slowed, Gizan and his men leaned into the walls. The doors opened and someone outside opened fire. The blasts hit the empty wall and Gizan returned fire, just aiming his weapon outside. Someone cried out and they were driven back, giving the invaders a chance to charge into the open space.

Terminals lined the walls and a step up near the center created a work space for five people. All around the middle dais, computer equipment created a barrier which inadvertently protected the defenders. The man who tried to take them out by firing into the elevator stood alone but dashed back to the safety of the central consoles.

A wild firefight broke out, forcing Gizan's people to take cover. One of them took a blow to the head and another was shot in the arm. They gave back twice what they received. Cries of agony echoed off the ceiling as the invading forces fired into the confined space. With nowhere to go and their position indefensible, the Pahxin forces were quickly defeated.

Gizan stepped out and motioned for his people to ensure their targets were dead. He approached the console, unmoved by the sound of blades sliding across flesh. Surely, their victims had died in the fight but he didn't want to take any chances. They might be up there for over half an hour and if so, that would be plenty of time for someone to recover and take a shot.

Monitors lined the space in front of him, twelve in all and Gizan filled them with security footage from around the station. He watched as his men made steady work of the defenders in the engineering section. They were fighting in a long corridor, taking cover in small inlets used for maintenance.

Those they were fighting made bold but foolish moves, dashing out when they should've remained back. Only two remained after a few moments and they refused to show themselves, knowing they would be killed.

Gizan tapped into the coms of his people. "You have two targets left and they are hiding at the end of your corridor. Their cover is sound so it would not be advisable to charge them. You will find the body of one of their soldiers nearby. I recommend you overload their weapon and use that to flush your targets out."

"Yes, sir!" One of them cried out, rushing forward to find the body. Several shots hit the ground around him but he continued on, unfazed by the attacks. He reached his destination and began fiddling with the firearm, keeping his head down. A moment later, he hurled it toward the defenders and dashed back to his cover.

Screams broke out and one of them dove to safety just as the weapon burst. The core didn't have enough charge left to kill the man but it did seem to daze him. Gizan's people charged and fired at the stunned individual, putting him down. One of them was rewarded with a shot to the side, a nonfatal blow that dropped them to the ground.

The others tore into the final defender, hitting him more than twenty times before they stopped.

Unnecessary, Gizan thought. At least they succeeded. "Prepare your charges but do not start them until I say."

"Dorin Station," a voice pumped through the overhead speakers. "This is Tella. Can you guys read me? What's going on? Why's the alarm going off? There's something wrong with coms too. I can't get a message out of the system. Did we have a reactor leak?"

One of the defending vessels. Gizan smirked as he prepared the weapons. The ships they needed to take were docked for various upgrades and repairs. Those flying around out there were in the way and needed to be dealt with. If they truly thought they were still dealing with their allies, then taking them out would not be overly difficult.

Gizan typed a message to them, explaining that their outgoing communications were experiencing a problem. Interference came from the reactor leak the commander feared. He requested they approach to send some help to replace some casualties they were experiencing. It only took a moment for them to comply.

Good thing they didn't notice our entrance into the system. My assault craft is truly a marvel.

The key to successfully dealing with the military craft involved holding off until the right moment to bring the weapons online and fire. As Gizan's targets drew closer, he noticed a com signal coming from the construction crews. They were asking what happened, looking for some assurance that they were safe.

Gizan locked down the doors, trapping the workers where they were. The docking clamps were also secured and could not be disengaged from the other side. Someone on the crews might be clever enough to break through and free themselves but by the time they thought to try, it would be too late.

He didn't answer their calls, turning his attention to the approaching ships that were an actual threat. The weapon's console indicated they were at extreme range. Come a little closer. I want this to wrap up quickly. Neither vessel had raised their shields. The trust remained even in the unusual circumstances.

"The station is secure." The report came through Gizan's earpiece and he smiled. "Detonators are set and charges are ready."

Gizan didn't reply but he brought the weapons online and fired into the destroyer. Massive cannons unleashed fury upon the larger of the two ships, tearing through the unshielded hull. Secondary explosions dotted the side and debris burst out in all directions. As it began to drift, the reactor went up and the whole craft was consumed in a golden bubble of flames.

A power surge in the scout indicated they were trying to bring their defenses online but they didn't have time. The station's weapons were vastly more powerful and far easier to redirect. Gizan fired again, annihilating the smaller ship with the first two shots. The rest were overkill, passing harmlessly through the chunks of molten hull.

The station is ours, Gizan thought. Time to make the best of it ... and rid ourselves of those unnecessary construction crews. He turned to his people. "Jettison the unfinished and damaged ships. When they are far enough away from the station, destroy them. Provide medical attention for our wounded and begin prepping what we can of our spoils.

"When our people arrive, I expect to have them acclimate and depart as soon as possible. We should be able to occupy two scouts and two destroyers. The next part of our mission will not be as simple, I assure you."

Gizan headed out to supervise the process. Killing everyone aboard wasn't the hard part. Getting people into place to commandeer their prizes, that would take some considerable administrative work.

Gizan's least favorite part of any operation.

***

The Gnosis returned home and immediate went about swapping out vehicles and getting their people cycled through to some ground time. Engineers came aboard and worked with Chief Engineer Nathaniel Webber to collaborate and ensure all ship systems were working properly.

They entered into discussions about the advancements coming their way and how best to implement them seamlessly without significant downtime. The second Orb helped them solidify a number of theories and they were in the simulation phase. Some of these advancements would end up in the new ship they were completing.

Others required more time to ensure they were safe.

Desmond and Vincent went through the records of volunteers who wanted to join the Gnosis. They had some people to replace, a couple who were transferring off and of course, those lost in the recent mission. Well over three dozen candidates applied and each of them wrote an enthusiastic letter to get on board.

"They're hungry for it," Vincent said. "Maybe they believe going into space will enhance their career."

Desmond shrugged. "I'm more inclined to believe they're all keenly aware that going into space with us is like putting your name in the history books. Others are going to come after us and very likely do more but no one can say they were the first to go into hyperspace and leave our solar system … or encounter an alien race."

"What's that tell you about these candidates?"

Desmond smirked. "That someone's talking who shouldn't. What we've been doing is secret. The fact we have so many means the rumor mill gave them hope."

One of the most important roles to fill was another Lieutenant for the marines. Desmond set up an appointment with Captain Darren Gabriel to sit down with the three men who might take the job. They'd be meeting with them at Gamma Alpha. Each of the men served there for over two years and their letters suggested they were ready for a change of pace.

They'll definitely get it on these cruises, Desmond thought. I can't imagine finding more action on Earth right now.

Military high command had yet to announce to the people of Earth what they were up to. As far as anyone was concerned, the Gnosis continued to fly training missions. There were conspiracies floating around, all generated from the usual suspects. The AIA was quelling the most probable of them but some would be proven true when a press conference was finally held.

Desmond wondered why they were waiting so long. Did they truly believe the planet would be swept up into a panic? Someone must've done some studies or polling to support the silent treatment but it seemed like getting the support of civilians would help a great deal. Especially for the men and women of the Gnosis who wanted to visit family.

Keeping quiet about their activities had to be difficult.

Speaking of civilians, one of the contractor companies would be meeting with Desmond on Earth. They were responsible for building some of the advanced systems the Gnosis used and they operated on Gamma Alpha under strict confidence. Reach's notification stated they wanted to have a chat with the man in charge of the ship.

Desmond didn't know why considering how little he could tell the person. His least favorite parts of the job involved making nice with vendors and going to lavish parties. Fortunately, they'd been too busy for that type of thing lately but of course, as soon as time permitted, he was thrown back into the fray.

I'd rather be facing down a Kalrawv ship again than try to beat around the bush with this civilian.

Desmond made his way to Gamma Alpha the next day and stowed his gear in his quarters before heading out to meet his full docket. Many of his meetings involved security planning for the admiral while he was aboard the ship. They were concerned about his safety though no one could specifically state why.

After six meetings, someone finally said they were worried about spies aboard the Gnosis who might try to disrupt the alien talks. Desmond found the notion absurd. No one had attempted to sabotage the ship and they had plenty of opportunities. Nevertheless, the accusation put a huge strain on psychological operations, who had to run profiles on every crew member.

Twenty men and women boarded the Gnosis so they could get the evaluations done before they left in only a few days so they ended up working some pretty crazy hours. Of course, psi-ops didn't have a whole lot to do during this potential conflict, considering they couldn't exactly study their opponents so Desmond didn't feel too bad.

The next morning, he and Captain Gabriel met in their conference room to interview the different lieutenants. Gabriel looked particularly severe with his dress uniform and buzzed haircut. His square jaw made him look like a character out of some kind of nineteen-fifties atomic science fiction movie and he carried himself with ramrod perfect posture.

"Morning, Darren," Desmond said. "How'd you find the trip?"

"Jeb's a good pilot," Darren replied with a scowl, "but the bastard doesn't need to fly so fast. We could've gotten down here five minutes later. I had half a mind to tell him so."

Desmond chuckled. "He saved a lot of lives with that crazy flying last mission."

"Yeah, when something's about to blow up, I'd take him any day but next time, I'm grabbing someone who isn't in such a damn hurry."

Their first interview arrived, a Lieutenant Yancy Lipkin. His record looked impeccable but in the first few minutes of their conversation, it became clear that he was too green for their needs. He'd graduated from the academy six months earlier and simply didn't have the field experience they needed to lead the team.

Desmond was thinking about an officer having to work with a man like Gunnery Sergeant Geoff Heathrow. Heading down to alien worlds was stressful enough without the men lacking trust in their leaders. When Yancy left, Darren completely agreed with Desmond's assessment. The young man needed time to develop.

Lieutenant Brent Fielding came in next, a twenty-seven-year-old soldier with a slightly less impressive academic record than Yancy but he came hot off a campaign taking on terrorists in Asia. He came with commendations from his superiors and positive testimonies from the men who were under his command as well.

"Welcome, Lieutenant," Darren said. "Why do you want to join the Gnosis?"

"Sir," Brent began, "I want to see the stars but more importantly, I'm the best person for the job."

Desmond's brows lifted. "Extrapolate on that. There are some pretty talented young people coming in here today. What makes you believe you're better?"

"I saw Yancy leave," Brent replied. "He's a fantastic bureaucrat. Understands every form we've ever made someone fill out. If you were having trouble with your quartermaster, I'd say you'd be crazy not to bring him on board. But the only trigger time he has involves a shooting range. He can shoot straight in simulations but he's never really been shot at."

"You think that's the key to success in our operations?" Darren asked. "The ability to shoot straight?"

"Keeping a cool head under fire is one of the most important things a soldier can do," Brent answered. "That and ensuring your men have a solid leader who will be right there with them in the thick of things. No one wants to follow a guy who's hesitant or doesn't know what to do next. I shook off combat jitters a long time ago."

"I've got a scenario," Darren said. "You're in a foreign facility far from any support. It's just you and four men. There are enemies on either side and the only way to take them out is to hit them in the head. Coms are down and you have to get to an LZ in thirty minutes or you'll be left behind.

"Add to this scenario that you still haven't finished your objective which is inside the facility somewhere. What do you do?"

"Get inside," Brent replied. "Conserve ammo with superior marksmanship, secure the cargo then head back outside using jump jets. We might not be able to kill our targets easily but I doubt they're going to enjoy having half a ton of armor plunging down on them as we hop through their ranks."

"Sounds like someone I know," Desmond muttered. "What's your tech experience? You good with computers?"

"I have an A rating with computer systems, analysis and access."

"Means you can hack them, right?" Darren asked.

"Yes, sir." Brent nodded once. "Essentially."

"Your record's pretty solid." Desmond looked it over again. "Let's get into some more semantic questions."

They quizzed the young man for another half hour, mostly about protocol and various regulations. Desmond wasn't surprised that he nailed every question though true to his words, he wasn't as knowledgeable about the red tape as Yancy. Still, he seemed like a solid choice and the kind of man who would be able to win the loyalty of the other soldiers.

When he left, Darren cleared his throat. "I think he'll be the one. Did you notice he didn't immediately go to the academy? He served as a sergeant before he applied for school. He'd already done a tour before he got a commission."

"Is that why he seems worldly?"

Darren nodded. "Definitely. I admit, I did the same. I fought in the eastern campaign of Russia before I went to school. It helped in more ways than you can imagine."

"I understand. I was a fighter pilot before I took the bridge of the Gnosis." Desmond hummed. "We need to talk to the third candidate and see how he compares. And here I was worried we would have to go back to the pool to find someone."

"Marine officers tend to be pretty solid," Darren said. "Not to say that other branches aren't that way but promotions are a lot harder with us."

Lieutenant Davy Prosser entered next, offering a crisp salute. Desmond peered at his record again and noted that he had a few demerits. One of them for public fighting and the other for intoxication. Both incidents were over eight months earlier but they didn't paint a positive picture, certainly not for a man about to go into space.

"I'm looking at your troubles here," Desmond said. "Would you like to speak to them?"

"A couple moments of stupidity, sir," Davy replied, "they won't be happening again."

"I'm sure you can see how we'd be concerned about this though."

Davy nodded. "Yes, sir."

"How much trigger time have you had?" Darren asked. "When was your last op?"

"A year ago," Davy said. "It was a training mission into Alaska."

"Any real combat?" Darren looked at his record again. "Off the books, I mean. I don't see anything official."

Davy shook his head. "No, sir. I'm ready though. I've been preparing for a real fight for five years now."

"Why do you want to go into space?" Desmond asked. "What's your motivation?"

"I think it's the future of humanity," Davy said. "I'd like to be part of it."

"You have a certification in astro navigation." Darren seemed impressed. "Why'd you go for that?"

"You never know when you might be stranded somewhere and need to get home."

"Fair point." Darren set the record aside and hit him with the same questions as the others. Davy seemed uninspired, as if he didn't want it as badly as the other two men. He might've been able to do the job but with the demerits, Desmond wasn't convinced. Besides, without the fire in his belly, he wouldn't be able to lead the men they already had.

Not effectively at least.

"Thank you, Lieutenant," Darren said. "You'll be informed of our decision in the morning. Dismissed."

Davy saluted. "Thank you, sir!" He spun on his heel and marched out.

"Seems like a clear winner to me," Desmond said. "We're going with Lieutenant Fielding, right?"

"I'd like to," Darren replied. "Lieutenant Prosser's father is on the military council, so we'll have to let the boy down easily ... Probably tell the old man before we do. But otherwise, yeah, I think we've got the right man waiting. Want me to draft up the orders?"

Desmond nodded. "I'll be happy to sign them. I'm glad we're good to go." He glanced at his computer and sighed. "If you don't mind, I'm going to take back some of my time to grab some food before the next meeting."

"Don't let me stop you, sir." Darren shook his hand and they parted ways. One of their bigger concerns was taken care of and now they only had to finish shoring up the security concerns. Once that was over, the Gnosis would be ready to leave and Desmond could finally get a little rest.

I barely remember what relaxing even is. Just another full day and I'll find out.

☐
Chapter 3

Cassie's computer chimed as a new meeting popped up and she groaned at the sender. Her superior, Beaumont Dulain, acted as the director of the AIA. Typically, she would've worked through a handler, someone far beneath a man of Dulain's stature but this situation warranted special attention.

Contacting aliens, traveling to foreign worlds and engaging in a new type of intrigue turned out to be events the AIA wanted direct involvement with. Cassie thought they'd relieve her once they finished their first mission. She possessed plenty of tech experience but hadn't been in the field nearly as much as others.

It's probably why they picked me. I can relate to the others easier and they don't smell an old spy who's there to steal their secrets. Indeed, her wide-eyed enthusiasm for her job must not have seemed like an act and in all honesty, it wasn't. However, considering the paranoia level of some people, she fully expected to be confronted sooner or later.

This time, Dulain wanted to meet her in a conference room instead of the hangar so the conversation must've been more 'official' than the last chat. What's he plan on putting on me now? The ability to start a war on Earth's behalf? He gave her a code during their previous talk which allowed her to take operational command of the Gnosis.

They wanted to ensure opportunities were taken. Cassie couldn't imagine an instance when she would take command or even tell Captain Bradford what to do. The man might've seemed like an easy going sort but there was something about him that suggested he would not take kindly to being usurped.

She told Desmond about the code, as Dulain suggested, and while he seemed good with the conversation, he wasn't entirely comfortable with it. Tipping her hand to him might've been a bad idea and maybe the captain complained. He might've raised enough of a stink to have her pulled from the operation. It would probably be fitting all things considered.

But she didn't want to leave. Not yet at least.

Cassie arrived a few minutes early and flopped down in one of the seats. She couldn't wait for the day to end so she could get some sleep and do something besides work on computers or talk about alien technology. Much as she loved both, the hours weighed on her and, like the others, she needed a decompression period.

Dulain showed up alone, closing the door behind him. The fact he lacked an entourage bothered her but she couldn't place why. He wore a fancy, retro suit with lapels and a black shirt underneath with gold trim along the seams. By contrast, she wore her white uniform that made her look like an especially stuffy lab technician.

The AIA has multiple looks depending on the situation. The uniform allows us to work closely with the military because they're comforted by that sort of thing. Others wear the fancy business outfits to give them some respectability but the real field types throw on whatever helps them blend in. Cassie remembered one of her classmates giving the assessment.

Back then, she thought they were just being dramatic and that clothing didn't nearly matter so much. After working in the AIA for a year, she realized how important appearance could be. Controlling a person's perception allowed one to exert power over them. Her innocent behavior on the Gnosis made the crew trust her, granted them security with her presence.

Had she been clever enough to be pretending, it would've been her choice to bring about that outcome.

"Senior Agent Alexander," Dulain said, "thank you for taking the time to meet with me. I've got some important news about your next mission."

"Yes, sir." Cassie somehow bit back a snippy comment. The director made her uncomfortable and her natural reaction involved rudeness.

"We know the Gnosis will be transporting Admiral Reach to meet with the Pahxin. He tried to keep us out of the loop by meeting you in space but we've had someone working as an aide for a while."

"Why would he want to keep the AIA out of this?"

"Reach is one of those old soldiers who thinks spies are always on the lookout for the next war," Dulain explained. "He believes that it's in our best interest to start trouble with the Pahxin so we can make ourselves useful. What he fails to realize is the best espionage is never reported, no one knows it happened and it prevents countless catastrophes in the process."

A line straight from one of the text books. Cassie nodded her response. "I understand."

"I'm going to give you her identity and if she requires support, she will be contacting you directly. She's a top priority asset and one of our best field operatives. There's a good chance you won't even interact but if you have to, if something goes down, then be prepared. Reach can be a stubborn bastard but we can't afford to lose him right now."

"Why is she being sent?" Cassie asked. "Is she a ... a bodyguard?"

"No," Dulain replied. "She's been giving us information from the admiral and now, this is our opportunity to gather some intelligence on the military capabilities of the Pahxin. Through her observations, we can determine just how outmatched we are and what we should plan to do about it."

"Are you sure that's wise?" Cassie asked. "If they find out ..."

"How would they?" Dulain shrugged. "As far as anyone but you knows, she's simply an aide. When she gets back and talks to us, she'll prove to be an especially observant one. Anyway, her name is Christina Dawson."

"This feels like unnecessary internal intrigue," Cassie said. "Can't we sit down and have a conversation? Tell him what's going on? He seems like a reasonable man. I've been to several meetings with him."

"Each time you've seen him, he's been in control. You're in his environment. Believe me, I've been in rooms where he is not the dominant force and you see a different individual emerge. We have to be cautious and we can't exert our will directly on him. Even if it saves his life. Now, I won't placate him if it means compromising the security of the Earth … but we're not there yet."

God, I hope we never get there. Cassie once again kept her thought to herself. "Thank you for the head's up. Is there something else we need to discuss?"

"I'd like to talk about the vision you had from the Orb. We have a theory about it."

"It happened while we were studying the second one. In fact, it showed me a glimpse of what likely happened to the planets we researched on this last time out."

"There are a couple of possibilities we've discerned," Dulain explained, "one, you may have found a new method of gathering historical data from the device. Or two, you've discovered the first steps we need to take toward updating our communications. Some are theorizing that the Orb may have a real time solution for chatting across great distances."

"I've heard some talk about that," Cassie said. "Doctor Harper's been working on it from what I understand. They talked about having to start over, that we've exhausted the extent of our current technology we built upon. I wouldn't be surprised. There comes a time when everything reaches a limit and needs to be overcome."

Dulain nodded, smiling at her comment. "Have you fully detailed your experience? I mean, everything. The sensation, the length of time, what you were doing exactly ... all of it?"

"Yes, I turned it over to the scientists." Cassie furrowed her brow, suddenly feeling unnerved. "Why?"

"I read a report which suggested some of the techs have tried to replicate what happened to you. They've done what you said you were doing and moved about the Orbs but none of them have experienced the same thing. We're going to need to recreate the experiment exactly the way you did before ... soon."

Cassie knew where he was going. "You want me to try again."

Dulain bowed his head for a moment. "Exactly."

"That ... seems a little crazy, sir. We won't be in controlled conditions."

"Ah, but you see ... the difference between the techs on Earth trying this and you is that you were in hyperspace. You see, I'm theorizing that there's some type of energy being spread around the internal part of the ship during faster-than-light travel. Something that allowed the Orb to connect with you."

"And they haven't figured out a way to simulate that," Cassie muttered, staring off into space. He might've been right. It actually made some sense. "Or you're saying they haven't even tried that yet."

"So far it hasn't seemed to dawn on them but it will when they exhaust all the other options." Dulain shrugged. "I'm confident they'll figure it out eventually but when you return, I want you to try proving my theory. My apologies, I occasionally like to get into the weeds."

"Okay ... I'll speak to Doctor Rindala about it."

"Maybe he even knows, but I'm getting the feeling that while they might've done more than scratch the surface they still haven't gone very deep. These things are an absolute treasure of information but we're incredibly cautious about how we claim it. I need you to be a little more daring while you're away from Earth. After all ... there's no one to complain. Much at least."

"They certainly aren't going to allow us to take one on board this time," Cassie said. "Not with the admiral and meeting a new race. We're trying to keep the ones we have safe."

"Yes, I know. I'm working on getting the new Orb transferred back to the Gnosis for our experiment. I should have an answer by the time you get back and we can see about tapping into the thing. Maybe you'll get better data as well, especially since everyone involved will know what we're trying to do. It won't be an accident."

"Next time then." Cassie sighed. "Something bothers me about all this. We know there are many Orbs out there and we know they were able to communicate at some point. Can they be used to spy on one another?"

Dulain shrugged. "Excellent point. One we should look into."

"Who's working on the virus?"

"Harper's people and a couple of ours." Dulain smiled. "You'd like to be on that team."

Cassie shook her head. "No, I would've been on that team. I feel I'm in the right spot."

"And you are." Dulain stood. "I believe that. Good luck and great work, Senior Agent. We'll talk again when you get back and see about pushing the boundaries of the Orb, huh? Should be very exciting."

Cassie watched him go, somewhat annoyed by how he used her new AIA rank. He emphasized the senior part as if reminding her of some obligation she already recognized and felt. The focus almost felt like a threat. Still, he gave her a great deal of latitude and didn't ask much. In fact, he pushed her to try things she would've thought would be forbidden.

I guess things could be worse. He could've told me I could start a war.

***

Desmond needed to get back aboard the Gnosis. They were going to depart Earth in less than fifteen hours and Vincent was left to finish all the preparations. However, Admiral Reach threw a meeting on his calendar, requiring him to visit Doctor Harper and Thayne on his way out.

This had better be exceptionally important. We really don't have time to be side tracked right now.

He figured whatever they had to say could've waited until they returned but then again, Admiral Reach rarely suggested a course of action that was completely out of place. As an old soldier with decades of experience, he'd proven to know what he was doing. High command gave him jurisdiction over the space program for a reason.

Gamma Alpha operated under his watchful gaze long before they had an enemy but once hostile aliens made themselves known, he turned out to be a fortuitous choice for leading the teams. Desmond knew him from his fighter pilot days and they'd gotten along fairly well back then.

When the Gnosis captain's chair opened, Desmond applied partially for the chance to go into space but ultimately to work closely with Reach again.

Doctor Harper saw him enter the lab and smiled brightly, waving. "Good morning, captain! Thank you for coming!"

"No problem," Desmond said. He took a moment to look over several tables laden with technology, most of which he'd never seen before. Terminals lined the walls, each blinking with multi-colored lights. Thayne stood at one of them, typing quickly on the touch screen, his eyes intense. "What's going on?"

"We've been studying the virus in the signal," Harper replied. "And I wanted to give you a quick update. So far, we've got some promising results when it comes to building a defense. Naturally, we're having to do everything in simulation but we're hopeful that, with some more time, we'll have a definitive method of fending it off."

"Excellent." Desmond nodded. He wondered if this was truly why they brought him in. Such a revelation could've been offered through a text message or over the com. "Was there anything else you needed to talk about?"

"I'm coming with you," Thayne said. "I just need to finish this final script ... I'm almost done."

"Yes, he's been working feverishly with me to nail down a realistic method of testing our defenses. Gil has also been helpful and he'll be staying here while you're away."

"That's what I heard." Desmond looked around. "I suppose he's a good choice considering his field of study. How has he taken to hanging around a couple Orbs?"

"Oh, like a child in a candy shop, I assure you." Harper snapped her fingers. "I forgot to tell you, we transported up some prototypes we've managed to test for the power armor your marines use. Chief Engineer Webber should be able to install them. They are short term personal shields, much like the Tol'An were using."

"Short term doesn't sound like them," Desmond said. "What's that mean?"

"Well, we haven't figured out how to make the power cores small enough, even for the armor, to keep them going longer." Harper shrugged. "These will take several shots from small arms and maybe two from something bigger. I figure it's a little advantage but one nonetheless. Any protection's better than none, right?"

"Sure." Desmond smirked. "Darren will be happy. Thanks."

"Oh, one more thing, I wanted to give you an update on our efforts with communications. Remember we talked about it on the ship but since then, we've discovered that the Orbs themselves could essentially be used to speak to one another through great distances. We've come up with a theory that those who built these must've found a way to send smaller Orbs with their spacefaring ships."

"I'm not sure about that," Thayne said. "They may have been traveling within Orbs themselves. Maybe not even using space vehicles but teleportation. It stands to reason considering these can do so much more than we ever thought possible."

"We've been debating that part, mostly because mine is practical and Thayne likes to … take leaps of logic to fulfill fantastic theories."

"They haven't been disproven," Thayne added.

"Anyway," Harper interrupted before he could go on. "It's been pretty interesting and we're currently exploring the option of how we would generate such a thing. Even if it only had a couple of uses, we'd be able to speak to you while you're out there and get messages back and forth. Maybe even send two or three along just to be safe."

"Definitely sounds useful." Desmond smirked at his next question because he knew the answer. "How long do you think before we'll be able to try such a thing?"

Harper's enthusiasm waned. "Unfortunately, we're at the very early stages of this thought process. Finding the data isn't proving as easy as we hoped but I'm confident we'll have some idea within a year … maybe less with two of them available. But you know how it goes, you have to dream it before you can make it."

"Of course." Desmond understood having a vision. It was imperative for leadership but he particularly admired the way scientists approached problems. They imagined a thing then found a way to make it happen and their objectives tended to have farther reaching ramifications than a combat scenario. "You ready, Thayne?"

"Yes, I am." Thayne grabbed a bag and approached. "Let's go."

"See you around, Doctor." Desmond waved to Harper before they left the room, heading for the hangar. "How do you feel about these negotiations with your people? Do you think they're going to be receptive to a partnership?"

"I believe so." Thayne seemed hesitant so Desmond pushed.

"What're the chances of them being less than genial?"

"Slim. Our people are proud but they are not monsters. We've made contact with several races, not all of which are our technological equals. Subjugation ended before we took to the stars." Thayne frowned. "I've caught up on your history and we have some similarities. Slavery, for example … and internal wars. We come from a common background."

"I hope that brings us together then."

"Understanding begins with similarity." Thayne's expression finally brightened. "We may be aliens to one another but I think my presence here has proven we can work together in a positive way to achieve results that are beneficial to all sides. And you have proven yourselves to be reasonable. After all, you saved my life."

"I would like to think you guys would've done the same," Desmond replied. "But after seeing the Kalrawv Group in action and facing down the Tol'An, I guess we could've had the misfortune of only encountering people like them."

"We had a run of bad luck with other planets for a while," Thayne said. "I recall several expeditions returning home with poor news about how they were received or discussing how they were told never to return. I often wondered if they were simply bad at diplomacy or if we were truly finding the worst curmudgeons in the galaxy."

"Maybe a little of both." Desmond wondered how humanity would've reacted to the Pahxin approaching them peacefully. He really had no idea what to expect. Would his people have assumed positive intent? He kind of doubted it. Cinema helped paint alien encounters as dangerous and apocalyptic.

He figured paranoia would've ruled over cautious optimism. Which is precisely why their missions had been secret. When they returned with news of the

Pahxin, he figured they would have a big press conference and let the world know about everything they discovered. Hopefully, with overwhelmingly positive evidence of a partnership, humanity could be happy about their actions.

I bet the polls will be on two sides of the spectrum, Desmond thought. There will always be those who don't believe an outside force can be reasoned with or trusted. Such individuals don't trust the government or military and never miss an opportunity to undermine the establishment due to their fear. We'll have to battle that behavior to stay unified.

"You look thoughtful," Thayne said as they left the building. The sun beat down on the open courtyard and Desmond felt sweat immediately form on his back. "Are you truly worried about this gathering?"

"I'm not sure what I am," Desmond replied. "Anxious maybe. I want it to be successful but I'm a soldier. I see danger, sometimes in places it doesn't necessarily exist. It screams at me to be cautious in any unknown situation. For example, your people have been to this station before and we haven't. Already we'll be at a disadvantage."

"It's a neutral space," Thayne said. "The people who run it are quite benevolent, I assure you. They have kept the peace for a very long time. You don't have to worry about something happening there. And our ships rarely fire first. They only do so on the terrorist organizations, like the Tol'An for example."

"I ... think that was meant to be comforting."

"It was."

"Nice try." Desmond smirked. They climbed a flight of stairs to the landing pad and boarded the waiting shuttle. He felt a sense of relief when he noticed the pilot was someone he didn't know. Thank God it's not Jeb. I'm not in the mood for his shenanigans. "Will you be going over with the admiral?"

Thayne shook his head. "No, I'm there to do the initial conversation when we arrive but the admiral and his staff will be going without me. I'll be briefing him along the way on several key points but our people made it clear they want to have a conversation that is natural between us. Though ... I must say it is a little ridiculous."

"Yeah?"

"I am telling the admiral everything I can to make this successful. Surely, my people know this."

"Speaking of which, are you planning on heading back with them?"

"I'll be speaking with their representative while we're there," Thayne said. "And I'll be making a case for staying with your people to help with the research. Believe me, part of the conversation will revolve around giving up one of your two Orbs, a point your people are dead against. If I can offer my services as a Pahxin representative, I might alleviate that pressure."

"That would be good. I know we're pretty set on keeping them."

"Even though you cannot do so from a military perspective, correct?"

Desmond hesitated but nodded. "Yes, I believe everyone's aware of that fact."

"We may want it, but we will not steal it." Thayne leaned back and took a deep breath as the ship took off. When they were airborne, he finished his thought. "Much as we would like to have the item, we learned long ago that taking things from a culture breeds nothing but ill will. Besides, what if you come up with creative solutions to problems we struggled with?"

"You think it might be advantageous to allow us to have both."

Thayne shrugged. "It very well could be. Who's to say? We've had it for a long time and we're still struggling with mysteries. Why not give you a chance? You're hungry for knowledge and extremely creative in your own rights. We never came up with the information about the virus, for example. That counts for something."

Desmond didn't disagree. More importantly, it didn't matter what either of them thought about the situation. The military high council would negotiate with the Pahxin and neither Orb would be on the table.

However, the humans might invite some scientists to help with the process.

At least Desmond hoped they'd be so reasonable. The problems everyone wanted to solve would benefit from as many intelligent eyes on them as possible. Qualified individuals, people who had far more years studying the devices would make the most sense. But sometimes, politics didn't care about such things. No one liked to compromise.

A com message buzzed his computer and Desmond brought it online. They were still a few minutes away from breaking atmosphere and then another ten minutes from docking with the ship. "Captain Bradford here."

"Good morning, sir," Vincent replied. "We see you're en route. The admiral arrived roughly five minutes ago. I've shown him to his quarters and he's settling in. He stated he'd like to be on the bridge when we go into hyperspace. After hearing about it so many times, he figures this is his chance to experience it for himself."

"He's going to be disappointed if he's hoping for bells and whistles," Desmond said. "Anyway, I anticipated that. I'm more curious about how much he wants to be involved in the day to day operations of the ship. Will he spend most of his time in his quarters or does he want to stay on the bridge?"

Vincent clicked his tongue. "I hadn't thought about that. Deacon's taking us out today and going into hyperspace. Do you think I should get Zach?"

"Did Zach work with Salina on the coordinates?"

"Yeah, our typical navigation procedures were followed. You know how our pilot is. He put in some hefty hours and I figured it isn't a grand event to fly for several hours and hit a couple buttons."

Desmond considered the situation for several moments. Vincent was correct. Just about anyone could perform the simple task of initiating hyperspace. However, they did have a VIP on board and that usually meant ensuring the best people were at their posts. Then again, Reach tended to be a down-to-earth type of leader so it was unlikely he'd be critical of the decision.

"Let's give Deacon his chance to shine," Desmond said. "Even if he isn't going to be doing anything too wild. It'll be good experience for him to do something basic under pressure and I'm sure as soon as he sees Reach sit down, he'll start sweating."

"Understood. We're scheduled to leave sixty minutes after you arrive. Is Doctor Rindala with you?"

"He is," Desmond replied. "I ran by the lab and got some news I'll share with you when we've got a quiet moment. I'm going to sign off. We're about to break atmosphere. Talk to you soon, Vincent. Bradford out."

Desmond tapped the computer and leaned back in his chair, taking a deep breath. Turbulence began to shake the ship, which struck him as odd that it took so long. The rattling only lasted a couple of minutes before everything went silent and they had achieved orbit. Experiencing such motion while in control didn't bother him but when someone else flew ...

He didn't care for being at the mercy of other pilots, regardless of how good.

"I trust everything's ready for us," Thayne said. "Your communication seemed to be about our departure?"

"Admiral Reach is already on board," Desmond explained. "I'm curious how he finds the ship so I'm anxious to get aboard. I was able to sneak up there yesterday for a quick inspection of my own but now I need to know how he did. In fact, I'm pretty sure he sent me to get you so he'd be able to check things out alone."

Thayne tilted his head. "Why would he do so?"

"Sometimes, people will say something different when their boss is around," Desmond said. "It's a tactic used by leaders the world over. Believe me, I've used it with a couple of my department heads when trying to understand how we're doing with a particular situation or problem. And before you ask, yes, I think it sounds like undermining too."

"So why do it?"

"As someone in charge, if you have to take point to solve an issue, then it's best to get your information from the horse's mouth."

Thayne's brows furrowed and he leaned back. "How do you extract such things from a beast? Is it painful?"

Desmond chuckled. "Sorry, it's just a phrase. It means you go to the source to find out what's going on and talk to the people directly. That way, there's no translation, no salving of the information. You know exactly what's happening. You can craft a solution because you personally heard what's going on."

"I see ... A personal investment works better for science too, I assure you." Thayne turned to look out the window. "Unfortunately for me, I became detached from the base level experiments. I was elevated to an administrator and suddenly was in charge of a team of scientists. It was not as fulfilling and often times, I didn't feel like I knew what they were doing."

"Then you have a good understanding of what I'm talking about," Desmond replied. "Men of action tend to have a hard time with the transition to leadership. You have to trust other people to do the work you'd been doing before. When you see them working inefficiently, for example, you have to remember you're there to coach them, not scold. So I get it."

"Yes! Oh, the trials we have faced." Thayne smiled at his own drama. "Thank you for this talk, Captain. I feel better."

"Good." Desmond smirked as well, looking out the window at the Gnosis. They would be there in a few minutes now and he could get to work. He felt an urgency to get aboard, a sense that he had a lot to do. Relax, he reminded himself. These few minutes might be the quietest you experience for a while. Take them in and enjoy it while you can.

Desmond drew a deep breath and settled into his seat. He might not be able to get all the way to relaxation but he could at least not stress about the workload ahead. There was plenty of time for that. Just then, he enjoyed the uncharacteristic silence of traveling through space without the constant demands on his time he could expect soon.

☐
Chapter 4

Cassie secured her quarters for departure and took a moment to go over her calendar throughout the flight to the space station. She had a mandatory rest period stuck in the middle of things but also a number of brief conversations with the engineering team and

Thayne. Vincent sent her a personal invite for a meal as well.

A knock on her door drew her attention and she double checked to see that she was free for that period. No one should've been contacting her, not without notice and she hadn't made enough friends on the ship to warrant a random visit. Considering they were less than a half hour out from dropping into hyperspace, she wondered if there might be some problem.

"Come in," Cassie called. She stood before the door opened, feeling ridiculously formal in her white uniform. The pants suddenly felt restrictive and the jacket gathered under her arms, pinching the skin. *I swear, I need to get one of the crew uniforms here and toss this fancy ass thing.*

An unfamiliar woman stood in her doorway, wearing the dress uniform of the military. The rank on her shoulder said she held the rank of major, a ground force designation and there were a couple of ribbons indicating she'd served at least three tours. Dark hair was gathered in a neat bun and her blue eyes scanned the room in an instant.

"Cassandra Alexander, I presume." The woman entered, clasping her hands behind her back. "I'm Major Christina Dawson. I believe you were informed about me."

"I was told you wouldn't likely make contact unless you needed to," Cassie said. "Is something the matter?"

"No," Christina shook her head. "But I like to put a face to the name before I have to rely on them in a pinch. Call me superstitious, but it's important in our line of work. Your support system literally becomes your life in many cases. This is an unknown situation to the extreme and the admiral has no idea just how dangerous it might become."

"I'm sure he has a good idea," Cassie replied. "He's spoken to Thayne … er … Doctor Rindala so he's got a solid understanding of what to expect from the Pahxin."

"You forget, I've been in those meetings and I can tell you with absolute certainty, our illustrious leader has no idea what he's walking into. Thayne isn't being as forthcoming as you'd like to believe."

"What do you mean?" Cassie fought hard to keep a neutral tone but she felt a sense of indignation hit her. Thayne was becoming something of a friend and she didn't like where the conversation was going. Did they truly doubt his honesty? His integrity? Had the AIA become too paranoid for their own good? "I've spent a lot of time with him. He seems on the level."

"Ah … Are you developing a friendship then?"

Cassie hesitated before answering. "I wouldn't say that."

"I see. You haven't been in the field before then."

"This is my first field assignment, yes."

Christina nodded. "The first rule you should've been told is to keep things professional. As soon as you find yourself falling into a personal relationship, your objectivity will falter. In the case of Doctor Rindala, you need to remember that he came to us after being under duress. He's not the most reliable of allies because he joined us out of absolute necessity."

"That doesn't mean he's against us," Cassie replied. "I believe he genuinely wants our people to cooperate."

"Perhaps so. But I've heard him give vague answers when it's fairly clear he could be more direct. Add to that the fact he's got a close friend who just happens to be a Pahxin criminal, one that we had to leave behind on Earth to avoid causing an incident or risk having to give the man up. Those are compelling facts to worry about."

"I see." Cassie chewed the inside of her cheek before continuing. "So ... is that what you're here to tell me? That I should be cautious?"

"No, I just wanted to meet the woman I'd be relying on if something terrible goes down on the station. I'm prepared to do whatever it takes to preserve the admiral ... and whoever else I can save. Let's ensure you have access to my personal com." Christina tapped at her computer. "You should be receiving an encrypted application."

Cassie frowned at her screen. "This is pretty intense. Who developed this code?"

"One of the newbies." Christina shrugged. "Seemed pretty robust so I decided to use it this time. Please ensure you can access my com before we leave the system. I'm not sure how many opportunities we'll have to meet after this."

"I will. It's going to take a while to install."

"I figured." Christina sighed, looking around the room again. "So ... how bad is hyperspace?"

Finally, something she doesn't seem to know everything about. "That depends on the situation," Cassie replied. "Sometimes, you barely notice but under duress, we've had to make some pretty crazy plunges. You mostly notice the first time."

"Ah ..."

Cassie noticed nerves playing at the corners of Christina's eyes. She tried to mask it but the signs were all there. "It won't be a big deal. We've done it plenty of times now so you probably won't even notice. In other words, all the scary tests have already been performed. It's becoming pretty routine."

"Good. I suppose you can be brave in many situations but flying faster than light ... traveling quicker than anything ever has in history ... It's pretty intimidating."

"I felt the same way our first time. The crew already did it twice before I came on board. Once to the outer reaches of our solar system and once to get back. They were pretty cool customers when we initiated the last couple trips, even when we were all about to die from the planetary core explosion."

"I read about that." Christina shook her head. "You guys sure know how to play it rough out here." Salina's voice announced that they would be initiating hyperspace in twenty minutes. "I'd better get to my quarters. Thanks for taking the time to talk to me. I really appreciate it and I look forward to working with you."

"You too." Cassie watched her go and flopped into a chair. The doubts Christina put in her head made her angry. She didn't want to worry about Thayne or any of the others for that matter. How long had it taken for Christina to become jaded? She didn't look all that old so it couldn't have taken too long.

Lord, I hope I don't follow that path. Becoming like her ... It would be like sacrificing one's humanity. And for what? Security? At the cost of indulging the ultimate paranoia. The AIA constantly looks for threats in the shadows but how long does it take before every motion looks dangerous? I'm walking a fine line here between loyalty and maintaining my sense of self.

This mission would not test Cassie, not terribly but she felt like a day would come when she'd be expected to take some kind of stand, make a decision she didn't agree with. When that time came, she wondered how she would handle it, both during the event and after. If she dreaded anything at all, it was the point of no return she knew was out there, waiting for her arrival.

***

Desmond took to the bridge on the verge of leaving hyperspace. Vincent sat beside him and the admiral took the seat normally occupied by Cassie. His aide, Christina Dawson, stood, holding the safety bar near the elevator. He didn't know why she needed to be present but he didn't bother to ask.

The departure from Earth went off without a hitch, despite Deacon's nerves. The young man practically trembled when he initiated the process and the admiral congratulated them all. Reach seemed impressed by their efficiency and he complimented them for their professionalism during what he considered the most frightening part of his career.

"I've read the reports about hyperspace," Reach said, "but I could not possibly imagine what it was like to go into it. Thank you all for your patience with my staff and I. Believe me, we all hold you in high regard for your bravery. Such a test … that first time you launched … must've been equal parts terrifying and exciting."

"Believe me, it was," Desmond replied. "But we were confident in the simulations and tests. Our own departure came after years of study. Those scientists wanted a victory."

Reach left them alone throughout the flight but he returned to be on hand when they were able to communicate with the Pahxin. Chances were good they would have communications the second they dropped out of hyperspace. Desmond was glad to relinquish the first contact responsibilities to his superior.

Much as I thought my soldiering days were over, after our last three missions, I've found myself leaning more heavily on my tactical skills. Desmond considered the situation for a moment, thinking back to why he joined the Gnosis in the first place. I thought I'd be an ambassador to other planets … even if there were no people to meet.

Fate had another plan for humanity and as they were plunged into a galaxy of conflict and dangerous organizations, Desmond adjusted easily into the combat role. He hoped it would not be necessary when they arrived at the station. Thayne made it clear any fighting between humanity and the Pahxin would not go well.

They have an entire fleet of warships and we've got one and a half. Their orbital defense vessels could travel about the solar system quickly enough but they lacked the ability to travel to distant stars. As the hyperdrive technology sophisticated, they would be retrofitted accordingly but until that time, the Gnosis was the only ship that could leave Sol.

So we have to be polite with these guys. I wonder how Reach was briefed by high command. Desmond tried to breach the subject to find out what their orders were but the admiral wouldn't discuss them. That made Desmond all the more nervous. If they were there strictly for a diplomatic mission, why keep any of it a secret?

I really hope we're not going to try to pull some BS here. Clever as we are, these people have dealt with many others in their time and they likely have a better grasp over not only the technology at their disposal but in deception as well. This is not the time for intrigue. We should be putting our cards on the table.

Desmond personally believed that handing over an Orb wouldn't have gone amiss. They could take one anyway so why not provide some good will right away? On the other side of the argument, he understood the desire to keep them both. After all, they were learning a great deal, more than ever before. Advances might come quicker.

And that could put us on an even ground with our new allies.

"I'm disengaging the drive," Zach said, "in thirty seconds."

Here we go.

Desmond noticed Admiral Reach's knuckles turning white a moment before the deck rattled and the viewscreen cranked on. Space opened before them and the other members of the bridge crew launched into action, compiling reports from the various departments throughout the ship. He waited patiently but he could tell his superior was anxious.

"We've worked out most of the little bugs." Desmond kept his voice low. "And engineering monitors all the major systems. Whatever we hear in a few moments should be fairly positive overall."

"What're you most concerned about?" Reach asked.

"Getting a hail from our potential allies," Desmond replied. "I want them to know it's us who just hopped into the area and that we're not here to cause trouble. Whether we're talking to the Pahxin government or the station administrators, I'd put announcing our presence at the very top of our priority list."

"All departments report green," Vincent said. "Zach, how close to our coordinates did we arrive?"

"We're thirty-thousand kilometers off," Zach sighed. "I thought we did a better job but I guess it's not too bad."

Desmond explained to Reach, "We've managed to come much closer to our planned arrival point. Regardless, we ensure we're aiming for a space which has plenty of room for massive miscalculations. That's why we've been so far out from Earth when we've returned from our missions."

Reach nodded. "Considering how far we just traveled, I'd say thirty-thousand kilometers sounds pretty reasonable."

"I can do better, sir," Zach said. "But thank you."

Desmond stood and joined Salina at her station, peering over her shoulder. She was scanning the area, staring at the screen intently. He waited for a few moments, trying to make sense of the figures dancing across the monitor on the right. When he couldn't make heads or tails of it, he finally just asked.

"What do you have?"

"I wish Cassie were up here," Salina replied. "She'd be able to help with some of these energy readings but other than those, we're definitely where we're supposed to be. Three hours to get to the station too so while we weren't where we wanted to be, at least we're closer to our end destination."

"Other ships in the area?"

"Not that I've detected yet." Salina hummed, gesturing to a blip on her screen. "The station is on my scans and it's pretty big … though not as large as the other place we visited. I'd say three hundred people could live there without feeling too cramped."

"Can you hail them from here?"

"Once we start moving," Salina turned to him, "I can get them on real time com in a half hour."

"Sounds like we've got a little time to kill then," Desmond said. "Zach, get us moving toward our destination. Vincent, let everyone know we'll be ready to get over to the station in just under four hours."

"I think I'll stick around," Reach added. "When we can speak to the station, I'd like to be on hand for the conversation. Christina, head down and let the rest of our party know when we'll be leaving. See about the shuttle and ensure we've got everything we need. I suppose we'll want to take a quick meal break before going as well."

"Yes, sir." Christina seemed hesitant to leave, which struck Desmond as odd. As an aide, she'd proven to be particularly clingy to Admiral Reach. She was a new addition to his staff, someone who joined him just before the trial tests of the Gnosis but as the program progressed, she became more prominent at his meetings.

I wonder what her deal is. Trying to get bumped up to colonel, I suppose. I'd love to take a look at her records. Desmond knew there was little chance of checking up on the admiral's personal staff but he felt curious. *Maybe a quick chat with her before we get back to Earth will reveal something. I'll try to set something up.*

Vincent spoke to the admiral, "Do you think this is going to be a straight forward conversation, sir?"

"I'm hoping so," Reach replied. "We've been preparing for this since we sent the message. It's time to see whether or not our efforts have been well spent. My advice is if we simply do all our jobs efficiently, we should come out with a new ally and be prepared to meet these various threats you've encountered with a unified front."

"I hope you're right, sir," Vincent said. "It would be a real tragedy if this went poorly."

"More than you realize, Commander." Reach narrowed his eyes, staring at the screen. "More than you realize."

***

Cassie entered the tech room where Thayne worked on one of the computers. She came up behind him and nudged his arm, offering a smile when he turned a confused look in her direction. They were less than a half hour from the station, preparing to board as soon as the Pahxin arrived.

"Your friends seem to be late," Cassie said.

Thayne shrugged. "A possibility. The distance between our home and here is much greater. Also, it is difficult to judge timing with faster-than-light travel … which you may find ironic, but it is the truth."

"I suppose." Cassie flopped down in a chair. "How concerned are you about all this?"

"Not very at all. They will either find common ground and work together or they will not. Negotiations may linger for a while but eventually, regardless of how this plays out, the two sides will become friends."

Cassie had listened to the initial conversation between Admiral Reach and the administrators of the station. It was formal, cordial and direct. They sent the rules of the station, which essentially amounted to variations of a single point: no violence. A brief history of the station came along with the rules.

The Gaeliran people who built the place lived on a nearby world which went through its own warlike phase. Fortunately, they got all that combat out of their systems before they took to the stars. When they contacted their neighbors for the first time, they were able to successfully negotiate peace and, as simple explorers, they went on their way.

Wars sprouted up between different factions throughout the years and many of them approached the Gaelirans, asking them to take sides. They never did, stating their total neutrality in hostile matters. This didn't go over well for them at first but the Gaelirans found a way to make it right.

They offered their space station up as a safe, neutral space for cultures to negotiate and after a couple times, it became a tradition. Their neutrality became respected rather than resented. A statistic in their introduction stated those who used their station for their gatherings signed peace treaties over war eighty-five percent of the time.

At the end of the digital brochure, Cassie found a list of reasons why other cultures have never attacked the Gaelirans or given them grief. While they forsook the warlike tendencies of their pasts, they maintained a fairly impressive vault of weaponry. These were used on those who broke the rules or threatened their people.

In the entire history of the station, they only had to exercise the power of their weapons once and even in that case, they simply disabled the offending craft. After that, no one else bothered to cause trouble in their areas. That bodes well for us but eighty-five percent conversion seems low. I guess blood can stay hot regardless of the decision to attend a peace talk.

"Have you ever been here before?" Cassie asked.

Thayne nodded. "Once, a long time ago. But it wasn't for a treaty. A science committee reserved the space. The Gaelirans have a voracious appetite for knowledge. I suspect they prefer such things over the negotiations they traditionally host. For example, you won't see them at the table for this but during our event? Dozens of them gathered."

"Nice." Cassie was about to ask another question when Salina's voice piped over the speakers.

"Attention, all hands to their stations. We have incoming ships and will be sending our VIP party to the station shortly. Please attend to your posts immediately."

Cassie stood and headed for the door. "See you later, Thayne."

"Good luck with the work up there. If you need anything, I will be down here monitoring the talks. I am issuing positive thoughts that this works out admirably for both sides."

"Me too, Thayne," Cassie replied, heading into the hall. She thought back to what Christina said about him and whether or not the woman was right concerning his loyalties. There seemed to be no reason for him to cause trouble and indeed, it behooved him for both sides to get along.

As a scholar of the Orbs, he would want to be close to them, not ostracized because the Pahxin and humanity didn't get along.

I guess we'll see soon enough.

***

Desmond scowled at the screen as four Pahxin vessels emerged from hyperspace not even twenty-thousand kilometers from the station. How did they make such a precise jump? What kind of navigation equipment would allow it? The questions didn't stem from idle curiosity. He was thinking tactically.

If the Pahxin can hop around to such close proximity, they can use FTL as a blitzkrieg-style attack method. We wouldn't have any chance to get defenses going in that regard.

They were larger than the Gnosis and a quick scan indicated they were heavily armed warships. Each of them carried enough firepower to level a small moon, putting them into an entirely different class than the ships they had encountered before. The Tol'An and Kalrawv Group couldn't field such vessels and Desmond was quietly grateful for it.

If these guys wanted to take something, they just would. This is part of the negotiation process. They're showing us what they've got so we can determine how far we feel like pushing them.

"Hail those ships," Reach said. "Get me on speaker and see if we can't have visual communication."

"Yes, sir," Salina replied. "They've acknowledged and are establishing a link now."

Cassie came onto the bridge and paused just in front of the door. Desmond nodded to her once before redirecting his attention back to the screen. The stars faded out and a figure appeared who could've been any other human. Brown hair was swept back from a high brow, brown eyes peered at them through a squint. He was clean shaven with narrow cheeks.

His uniform, black with silver piping on the seams, could only be seen from the middle of his chest up but the collar was buttoned high on his neck. When he spoke, the computer automatically translated his words for them so they only heard the mechanical voice. The effect was somewhat eerie since all tone was lost in the English words coming from the speakers.

"Greetings, humans. I am Captain Ulian Hataran. Our ambassador will be heading to the Gaeliran station momentarily. Are you prepared for the meeting?"

"We are," Admiral Reach replied. "Is there anything you need from us before we begin the process?"

"No. Merely note that this sector is a peaceful one. Any hostilities will be met with extreme force from us … or our hosts. And believe me, I have seen the might of the Gaelirans in simulation. No one wishes to push them."

"We have no intention of indulging any hostilities," Reach said. "We are here to negotiate for peace and a union between our two people. I believe this will be beneficial. I'd like to introduce you to the commander of this vessel, Captain Desmond Bradford. He will be holding the ship down while I'm on the station."

"Yes, I see." Ulian frowned. "We will be in touch. Ulian out."

The screen went dark, shifting to a view of the station and stars again. "Charming," Vincent muttered. "Maybe they just don't translate well."

"Soldiers," Desmond said. "I'm not taking it personally." He turned to Reach. "Seems like we're ready to get this show started. Shuttle should be prepped."

"Wish us luck, Captain." Reach nodded and headed for the elevator. "Do ensure we don't engage in any hostilities."

Desmond nearly dropped a snarky reply but merely nodded, returning to his seat. Captain Hataran likely found himself in a position where he didn't know why they were bothering to negotiate with humanity. If he understood the situation, if he had been briefed on the Orbs, then he might have offered a military solution to get at least one of them back.

Considering they were all out there at the Gaeliran station, their government decided on a peaceful course of action. Still, Desmond understood the notion. The simplest path often proved to be the quickest. Depending on how desperate they were to acquire one of the Orbs, violence made the most sense.

"Salina." Desmond turned in his seat again. "I trust you're ready to monitor the proceedings."

"Yes, sir. I'm on it."

Cassie sat down and logged in. "I'll get a decent scan going of the Pahxin vessels. Maybe we can learn something from how they're put together ... weapon placements, power core ... Anything would be of value."

"Let's make sure they're okay with it," Vincent said. "Last thing we need is for them to get all huffy 'cause we're prying."

***

Christina spent more time in boring meetings than she could possibly remember. The admiral's duties took him through the paces of such things frequently. Unfortunately, meeting with aliens didn't prove to be any different. Two bodyguards accompanied them and on the flight over, they proved to be terribly nervous.

But the negotiations themselves would likely be just another meeting involving a whole lot of talk.

The accommodations were nice enough. When they arrived in the hangar, it looked much like their own but upon departure, they found themselves walking down a hallway with dark wood paneled walls at the top and some kind of bone colored material at the bottom. The floor was carpeted and it felt like a resort.

Not at all what Christina thought of when she considered a space station.

The Gealirans proved to look much like humans but they kept their heads shaved. Their eyes were set a bit wider and their lips were thin. It gave them a cartoon like experience but they'd taken the time to learn

English, though it was thickly accented with emphasis on the vowels.

The admiral's party was led to a conference room with refreshments lining the wall and a massive table with several chairs. The Pahxin arrived moments later, dressed all in black. Such severe appearances surprised Christina but the color probably didn't mean the same thing to them.

She wore her black dress coat, white pants and a white blouse. It was what passed for a dress uniform in the army. Admiral Reach wore the same but he had more ribbons and awards than she did. The bodyguards came in loose fitting bodysuits, still nice but more utility. If they needed to do their jobs, they wouldn't be hampered by fancy outfits.

At least this stupidity doesn't include heels. I'll ditch the jacket if something goes down and make something happen.

Christina introduced herself to the primary bodyguard of the Pahxin, a man named 'Lothan'. He could speak decent English and seemed friendly enough but he definitely kept a wary eye on her party. The bigwigs found their seats and she headed over to stand behind the admiral.

The Pahxin ambassador stepped forward and bowed to Admiral Reach before greeting him in decent English. "Greetings. My name is Raeka Vinn, ambassador of my people. I come authorized to speak on my culture's behalf and to express our excitement to work closely with you in these negotiations."

"Thank you," Reach replied, bowing his head in return. "I'm Admiral Garlan Reach and I look forward to ensuring we find common ground and a platform to build a solid relationship upon."

They carried on with a few more pleasantries before relying on the computer translators but the effort they made was worth noting. Christina wondered if they should've attempted to do the same. They had Doctor Rindala around and the Orbs would've provided enough data to learn a few lines in their language.

Regardless, she took mental notes of everything that transpired so she could report back to the AIA later. This meeting was an absolute gold mine of information, from the way the bodyguards carried themselves to the uniforms to the speech patterns and body language. As the first peaceful gathering with an alien species, it provided them with a wealth of opportunities.

An hour passed where things seemed to be going well when an alarm went off, a high pitch, staccato beeping that continually blared overhead. God, let that be some kind of meal time alert. Christina's whole body tensed as she waited for some explanation. The Pahxin seemed nervous as well and the admiral held his hands up to try and placate them.

"Perhaps we should contact our ships to see what's going on." He turned to Christina. "Can you call the Gnosis?"

"I'm on it." Christina paced away, lifting her computer. She tapped the screen but noticed there was no connection. Something was jamming her. Internal? External? What the hell? Not even the advanced tech she had from the AIA could get through. Were the Pahxin pulling something?

As she turned, she noticed they were experiencing the same challenge. *Okay, so we've got a bigger problem.*

"Admiral," Christina said, "I believe we should get you to the shuttle right away."

"But we're right in the middle of this." Reach shook his head. "I think we'll wait to see what's going on."

"That might be too late." Christina scowled, turning to Lothan. She used her computer to help translate. "Do you have any idea what's going on?"

"I am afraid I do not," Lothan replied in slow English. "We cannot reach our ships and the Gaelirans have stated they are also unable to speak with their people."

At least the peace lovers haven't gone crazy just yet. Christina considered the options but Reach was set on waiting. *I guess we'll let the trouble come to us.* She assigned the bodyguards to the door they came in through and they locked it. The Pahxin watched the other one. They didn't even have windows to peer out and see what was going on.

Blinded and waiting for something to go down. Excellent. I hope this is some kind of false alarm. For all our sakes.

☐

Chapter 5

Desmond studied the scans Salina and Cassie pulled of the Pahxin vessels. They received permission to do so though their potential allies seemed reluctant. Some aspects of their vessels matched the Gnosis while others went in radically different directions. The largest departure seemed to be in their propulsion.

Pahxin scientists successfully completed reactionless drives, engines that propelled them without the need for thrust. This gave them a high degree of maneuverability and consistent motion. Furthermore, their power cores used some other type of material, one the Gnosis scanners couldn't easily identify.

Must be something native to their home world.

Regardless, they still maintained rear thrusters. Desmond figured they kept them as a sort of backup, in the event something happened to their fancier drive. Of course, they might also use it for combat to get a little extra speed. I'd love to see this thing in action.

Desmond was about to get into their weapons when Salina gasped. He glanced in her direction, brows raised. The woman rarely seemed surprised so whatever she saw had to be serious. He gave her a moment to study her screen as her hands flew over the controls. When she finished, she turned sharply in her seat.

"Captain, I've picked up multiple incoming ships." Salina gestured to the screen. "They're moving on us fast."

"What?" Desmond scowled. "Do you have an ID?"

"I believe so … at least for two of them. They appear to be the Tol'An. I've matched silhouettes to the attack on Earth. These are definitely the same."

"Get Ulian on the com." Desmond stood as the connection established. "I assume you guys see the incoming?"

"We do," Ulian replied. "It appears they have managed to commandeer two of our destroyers and two scouts. We'll take care of it. If these scum think they can disrupt these talks, then we shall have to convince them otherwise. Ensure that you are out of the way."

Desmond glanced at his computer and counted six Tol'An ships. "They outnumber you. I think we should help."

"If you genuinely believe you can do more than be in the way, then by all means engage the enemy."

Ulian offered a thin smile. "Do ensure your pilots know which Pahxin to shoot. Ulian out."

"He's a real piece of work!" Vincent shook his head. "I'll get our fighters ready. We should have them out in less than five minutes."

"Good." Desmond turned to Zach. "Ready the weapons and sound battle stations. I can't believe these guys would pull something like this. They can't possibly think they can win. What's their angle?"

"Maybe they simply want to cause some damage," Vincent said. "It's a good place to try it."

"More likely," Cassie interjected, "they're hoping to cause some kind of conflict between our two people. If they could start a war between the Pahxin and Earth, then we'd do the work for them. I'm guessing their biggest obstacles are all parked here right now."

Salina sighed. "If you're right, then they can't leave any survivors. Not even the Gaelirans."

"But I thought those guys were super scary," Vincent replied. "At least, that's what I read about them."

"I suppose it depends on if they get attacked," Desmond said. "Maybe the Tol'An think they won't say anything. Who knows? Regardless, let's contact the admins of that station and tell them what's going on. I'm pretty sure they'll want to know why we're about to start blasting away at enemy ships in the middle of a peace summit."

***

Gizan Relik stood on the bridge of the Tol'An assault craft, staring intently at the station before them. His plan remained simple: get aboard the station, kidnap the dignitaries and depart. The other ships in his small fleet would be enough of a match for the defenders to keep them busy while he worked.

There will be much death today and not even the Gaelirans will be able to prevent it.

He knew about their fanatical devotion to neutrality. They defended it like an animal might protect its offspring. However, they were not prepared to contend with a quick assault, a daring boarding action. His well-trained units would easily cut a swath through any defenders but the real threat remained with the bodyguards of his targets.

Pahxin men and women would be prepared to fight to the death to defend their ambassador. Gizan didn't know what to expect from the humans but after hearing how they had trounced the Tol'An both at their home world and later when they snatched the Trindisha from their clutches, he knew not to underestimate them.

I will cut them down regardless.

The pilot broke his reverie, "We will be able to board in a few moments, sir."

"Attach yourself to the following bay," Gizan said, programming coordinates into the computer. "That will be the easiest port to break through. A maintenance hatch that is not comfortable for the regular people they admit to the station. Is our expert prepared?"

"I am, sir," the voice behind him came from a highly trained individual who had hacked into Pahxin systems many times in the past. "I can begin the process shortly so it's ready to open upon our arrival."

"Excellent. Ensure that it is. We will not have time to wait. The faster we work, the less time their security will have to settle in." Gizan's eyes narrowed. "Fire to kill. We cannot allow any of them to survive. Our departure will be made in much more haste than our arrival, I absolutely assure you."

"Master," the pilot spoke. "What about the fighters? How are we going to evade them?"

"That's what the rest of the ships are for," Gizan said. "You do not worry about them or their duties. Our sole purpose is getting on that station, collecting our cargo and getting off. Anything else is a mere bonus. If the Pahxin lose their warships here, so much the better but the human ship ... I believe that is their only vessel capable of hyperspace."

"Should we not prioritize that as a target?" The pilot asked.

"No. It would be a benefit to our cause, but we have not been sent for that. Besides, we did not come equipped for such a conflict. This is about surprise. And when they see us on that station, I promise you the terror and shock will be quite real. Prepare yourselves. We are nearly there."

***

Squadron Leader Dennis Arden stared straight ahead as he and his team raced to meet the enemy. His scanner showed dozens of Pahxin fighters bursting from the four warships not far off, and they adopted a scattered formation. His own people used a vanguard but they were spaced far apart to avoid any area attacks by the larger enemy vessels.

None of them thought they'd be called upon for this particular mission. All the pilots were in the rec room when the alarm went off requiring everyone to get to their battle stations. At first, Dennis was convinced it was a drill but the timing didn't make sense. There was no way that Captain Bradford would put them through paces in such a delicate time.

If the Pahxin misinterpreted what their scans told them, it could've easily led to a fight.

The quick briefing stated they would be meeting the Tol'An again. It was the only good news about the scramble. Most of the Gnosis crew wanted another shot at them after the bastards attacked Earth but their second mission didn't involve them at all. Much as the soldiers wanted to wage war against them, one ship wouldn't be enough.

Even if we beat their asses when we got the second Orb. Dennis tried not to be arrogant about their victory but it was hard not to feel a little smug. Yes, they experienced some losses but not before they sent them packing a second time. *Maybe if they wouldn't have divided their forces, we would've had a harder time tearing them up.*

"We're approaching the first fighter screen," Flight Lieutenant Shane Goring called out. The younger man had been working toward a promotion and Dennis was giving him more responsibilities. While he wasn't technically leading Mustang squadron on the mission they were currently on, he was operationally in charge for the moment. "Prepare yourselves."

Dennis checked his shields and noted they were at full strength. Weapons were hot and ready to go. He checked the distance before he'd be in firing range and tensed up. Ten seconds. The enemy ships lit up, their weapons powering on for the first attack. Pahxin ships arrived moments before them and chaos erupted some distance to the left.

That's a lot more ships than I thought we'd face, Dennis thought. He was grateful for the help but as they zoomed in with Charger squadron at their side, he realized that had they been alone, they would've been hopelessly outnumbered. *The initial scans are showing* we'd be looking at three to one and we fielded twelve ships!

A beam sizzled his shields with a near miss, bringing Dennis fully back to the moment. He fired a burst with his guns then initiated his top thrusters to drop low. The attack connected with a target, the metal burning up in the enemy's shields.

They flew by one another, each ship a momentary blur before Dennis and Shane banked hard to the left and came around to find a firing solution. All around them, the dogfighting became intense, violent dances taking place as pilots struggled to gain an advantage. Weapons fire lit up the darkness around them, potshots meant to misdirect targets into better positions.

Bright flashes winked all around them as different vessels began exchanging beam shots. Com chatter increased. Charger squadron dove into some immediate action, calling their targets as they began blasting away. Despite all the activity, it felt less chaotic somehow, more controlled. Perhaps it was the fact they were flying with allies.

Dennis picked a pair of ships for them to focus on and they sped toward them. The targets were trying to line up shots on two ships from Charger squadron but their prey proved too wily. "Computer's trying to acquire a target," Shane said. "What do you think about missiles? Might chase them away from our allies."

"Hm." Dennis shook his head. "No. A proximity explosion to the other ships might be enough to cause some damage. Let's stick to beam weapons and make this attack surgical. I'm going to take a shot at the one on the right. It might push him into your line of sight. Get ready ... You might only have a moment."

Dennis spun to the right for a better angle and unleashed his beam weapons, depressing the trigger several times to break up the attack into bursts. They flew toward the enemy and he spun wildly away, the corona from his engines blurring together as he evaded. Just as he righted himself, Shane fired.

Shields shattered, tiny electric lines appearing in space before vanishing in a bright flash. The second and third hits pounded into the metal and melted the fuselage, shutting down the engines. A brief tumble took the ship a good fifty meters away from his allies before the vessel exploded in an orange-purple ball.

"Scratch one," Shane called. "Good show."

"Not done yet." Dennis veered to the left to avoid a retaliatory attack and once again flew by another target. Charger was hot on the enemy's tail, firing guns the whole time. Shane moved to support him and Dennis caught up as well, lining up for a shot. The three of them synced up and unleashed all at the same time.

Each attack hit the rear of the vessel as it attempted to escape. Dennis didn't even see the shields go down this time. The ship was obliterated instantly, pieces and debris scattering in all directions.

Not bad so far, Dennis thought. He looked around, his heart nearly stopping in his chest as he saw one of the enemies dashing toward his left side. A direct hit caught him as he initiated a dive and an alarm went off in the cockpit. "Alert," the computer stated in a calm voice. "Alert. Shields down to fifteen percent. I repeat …"

"I heard you," Dennis grumbled. "I've been hit … Systems check isn't done so I don't know how bad it is."

"Can you still maneuver?" Shane asked. "Wow, that guy who got you is coming back around. He wants to finish the job."

"A little help then?"

"Don't worry … I've got it." Shane hesitated for a moment and light flashed over Dennis's controls, illuminating the cockpit. "There you go. He's done."

"Automated repair has kicked in to fix my shield generator." Dennis checked the diagnostic quickly. "It overheated. Crap!"

"Fall back and give it some time," Shane said. "We can hold this rabble for a few moments."

Dennis noticed that the larger ships were heading toward the Gnosis and the Pahxin warships. He counted seven in all but they looked dangerous. His scanner didn't indicate what they were packing but it must've been potent if they were willing to charge in without even slowing down.

I wonder what they have up their sleeves that makes them think they can pull this off. Dennis frowned and kicked on his afterburner, taking himself out of the dance floor of combat. Dogfighting continued all around him, ships exploding here and there while others merely took damage. He saw the tally on his own screen as his allies suffered minor damage.

The Pahxin fighters seemed to be doing a good job but they'd at least lost three of their number already. They entered the battle with a larger force but Dennis didn't think they could afford heavy casualties. Maybe it was just the way the humans thought about death that brought the thought to mind but either way, their newfound allies were no joke when it came to combat.

Dennis pulled away from the fighting only to find he had one of the enemy ships hot on his tail. *Are you kidding me?* He initiated evasive maneuvers, trying to get further away from the opponent. If he led it back toward the Gnosis, automated defenses might save his life but it was a long trip and they'd have some of their own problems to deal with.

A couple blasts flew by him to the left then over his head. He continued to move erratically, trying to ensure he was an impossible target to hit. "I could use a little help over here if anyone's close by!" He spoke louder than he intended to over the tactical com net. "Sorry to be insistent."

"I'm on my way," Shane said. "But it'll be a minute."

"Settle down, humans," a heavily accented woman's voice broke over the com. "I am coming."

Dennis saw one of the Pahxin ships flying toward him on the right. His opponent nearly got him with another shot and he pulled hard on the stick, trying to draw closer to his potential savior. He gritted his teeth as the inertial dampeners fought to keep up with his motions. Even with all his fancy flying, he couldn't shake his pursuer.

"Warning, missile lock." The computer let him know the enemy was about to drop some heavier ordnance on him and he cursed his luck. "Prepare for countermeasures."

"Don't bother," the woman said. "I've got this." She fired her weapons, turning the enemy ship into ash in an instant. There wasn't even an explosion. It simply turned into debris and was gone.

Dennis swallowed hard, glancing over his shoulder then turning back to look at the woman's ship. "How the hell did you do that?"

"That's our disruptor beam," she replied. "What is your name?"

"Dennis Arden ... Squadron Leader of Mustang."

"I am Dala Ahnshyr. Stick with me and I will protect you while your shields repair. We do not have time so divert power as you can, human. We must re-enter the fray and stop these criminals before they cause more trouble."

"Working on it," Dennis muttered. "Shane, I've got this back here. Stick with the action nearest you. I'll be back as soon as I can."

With the kind of weapons these Pahxin are sporting, I doubt we'll be in this brawl for long. Lord, they're more powerful than we thought. Of course, there has to be some reason they haven't finished these criminals off. I only hope we don't find out what it is today.

***

Cassie tried desperately to break through the jamming signal so she could communicate with the station. Salina turned her attention to coordinating their ships. Though they couldn't talk to the admiral's party, they could still chat amongst themselves. She took her place in the combat mission, leaving the tech stuff up for grabs.

I can't even tell the Gaelirans that we're not responsible for this, Cassie thought. I hope they understand and know how to read the Tol'An signatures.

If the station was under total lockdown for communications, they probably couldn't reach out o the nearby planet for assistance or support. That meant the Gnosis and the Pahxin ships were the only ones who had any chance of engaging the enemy and stopping them in a timely fashion. Unless our allies reached out to the Gaeliran high command.

Cassie tried to hail one of the ships and got them on the line a few moments later. A man's haughty voice took the line but his strange language was translated into the toneless computer articulation. "What do you need, Gnosis?"

"Have you informed the Gaelirans of what is happening?"

"We cannot get through the interference," came the reply. "And the planet is not answering either. It seems the Tol'An have figured out how to target jamming signals while not wasting the energy to hit the entire system. That is why we can still talk to our people … and you it seems."

"Understood. I'm working on an algorithm now that should get us in touch with our people. I'll share it the moment I'm done."

"If such a thing works," even the computer sounded snooty, "we would be happy to see it but we will not hold our breath. Good luck."

Cassie frowned. Okay, check. We're pretty much monkeys to these people. Good to know. Thayne never showed such an attitude so she wondered where it came from. The Pahxin had encountered other creatures throughout the galaxy. Had they treated them all in such a way? Did each encounter they had involve their potential allies having to prove themselves?

Perhaps these particular Pahxin hadn't heard about what the Gnosis had already accomplished. Whether or not the Gnosis needed to strive toward some expectations shouldn't have mattered. It seemed odd that anyone would lack all faith in humanity, all things considered. Thayne's message must've spoken of how they performed against the Tol'An before.

Why would the Pahxin military act so superior given the circumstances?

Cassie focused on the work at hand but before she could progress, Salina appeared behind her, leaning close. "I've picked up a ship flying straight for the station. Can you confirm my scan? I'm picking up a strange reading about it … something I'm not sure what to make of."

"Okay." Cassie peered at the screen and frowned. The smaller vessel was moving as fast as a missile and it emanated a strange signal. When she traced it, a realization dawned on her. "They're trying to open the doors remotely. That's what you're picking up. They've accessed the Gaeliran network."

"So they're heading inside." Salina shook her head. "They are either trying to kill the dignitaries or capture them."

"I would support that assertion." Cassie gestured to her terminal. "I have to get a connection to the admiral. We need to tell them what's going on so they know help is on the way."

"If we can get them there." Salina turned away. "Captain, we have picked up a small vessel attempting to board the station. It looks likely they will succeed. Recommend we prepare the marines to assist and extract Admiral Reach."

"Agreed." Desmond nudged Vincent. "Make that happen. We've got that new lieutenant on board. I'm sure he's itching to get out there and prove himself."

"Yes, sir." Vincent started making the arrangements.

"We need to get a shuttle through this mess." Desmond hummed. "I'm sure they'll grab Jeb. He's insane enough to make it."

"The capital ships are almost in range," Zach said.

"Sir," Salina announced. "Captain Ulian is hailing us."

"Put it on the screen."

***

"Captain Bradford," Ulian began without preamble. "Much as I do not believe your people are ready for intergalactic affairs, I would rather work with you than have you be a hindrance. It seems our pilots are already cooperating which is good. Now, I need you to understand the position we're about to be in and how to proceed."

"I'm not sure what you mean."

"This is not a typical Tol'An attack force," Ulian explained. "They have never come at us head on. Their preferred tactic involves hit and run. Harassment. There's a danger here. I'm sure you have noticed their attempt to board the station?"

"Yes, we're sending people to help now."

"Oh?" Ulian seemed surprised. "Good. I will not send additional forces then. The problem with station fighting is that it can be close quarters. Smaller forces tend to work the best. The most fighters the Tol'An could possibly field with their vessel is fifteen and that's if they are practically sitting on one another."

"Our people should be able to handle them." Desmond hesitated a moment. "Do you think they're planning on fighting to the last man here or do they have something else in mind?"

"If I was to guess, they only care about distracting us long enough to do their work on the station." Ulian shrugged. "I believe we can stop them and cripple their forces by taking out these ships. Please hold to the right flank and we will attack both down the middle and to the left. Can you manage this?"

Desmond had half a mind to protest the question but he knew there wasn't time. The man would be terse given the circumstances. They were about to conduct a major military action and like it or not, Ulian had more experience. I need to trust his judgement and assume positive intent.

"Yes," Desmond replied. "We'll hold our end. Let us know if you need additional support. Our fighters are engaged there though so ensure your friend or foe is working before you do anything too crazy."

"We understand this type of combat, Captain." Ulian offered a thin smile. "I believe we can now show you exactly how it is done. Ulian out."

"That guy has nerve." Vincent shook his head. "I've briefed the marines and they're hurrying to get out of here. I expect they'll be in the air inside of ten minutes."

"I hope they can go faster than that," Desmond said. "I doubt the people on the station have so long … unless I'm seriously underestimating the Gaelirans."

***

You might be underestimating the bodyguards, Cassie thought. Or Christina. If she's truly as good as Dulain said, she might be able to get Reach out of there.

The signal to the station proved to be particularly challenging to overcome. Every algorithm Cassie tried either made the interference worse or did nothing at all. She analyzed it again, looking for ways to replicate it when she realized it was changing subtly every time she tried to break through.

What's the source? Cassie followed it to one of the capital ships. There you are. A quick scan indicated it was the smaller Tol'An vessel. The weapons weren't as potent but it carried heavy defenses and probably fielded the majority of the fighters that were causing trouble at the moment. Taking them down isn't likely but maybe I can disrupt them at the source.

Cassie painted the target and considered her next move. There were a few options but one of them involved calling in the bombers. Considering the heavy action going on outside, it might be unnecessarily dangerous. The marines would be heading over there regardless but once they got on board, they'd be unable to communicate.

Maybe I can jam them back. The thought held some merit and she brought up an application, blasting the enemy ship with a tremendous amount of static. The whole process took less than a minute but it ultimately failed to provide the desired result. Their signal remained strong.

Are you kidding me? How? A scan of the activity showed their shields deflected it. Oh. So I can't even get through their defenses. Hm. Maybe if I flood the area around that ship but I'll need a probe to broadcast the signal. Otherwise, I'll be sending it straight through all our forces which would cause trouble with our own coms.

"Captain, I need to launch a probe at the enemies," Cassie announced. "I might be able to disrupt that signal if I can."

"Go for it," Desmond replied without looking back at her. "If it makes it through, that'll be a miracle."

"It only has to get close." Cassie prayed she was right as she prepped the device and set the coordinates. "Launching now." She tapped the touch screen harder than she needed to, eyes glued to her screen. The probe flew of, plunging toward the heavy action between the various pilots.

She hoped it was small enough to not to be noticed. It would take it nearly ten minutes to get through the action then another five to arrive at her target. Once there, she could initiate her application but even that wasn't a guarantee. It's better than nothing, I guess. We have to try something … I just hope this isn't all over before it gets there.

***

Gizan waited for the doors to his ship to open, standing off to the side. If someone waited to fire on them again, he would not be the first one to be shot. When nothing happened, one of his men chuckled. "It appears the Gaelirans are staying true to their neutrality. There's no one out there."

"Then let us commence with the mission." Gizan led the way, stepping out into the maintenance corridor. He had been to the station before, long ago as a younger man. As a bodyguard for a dignitary, he wandered the halls during a week-long negotiation. Though he didn't remember the event, he recalled the layout quite well. "Follow me."

Gizan approached the next door and tapped the button, shaking his head when it opened immediately. *They lock nothing. These fools do not care about security.* He entered the next room, a well-appointed affair with dark paneled walls and carpet on the floors. A Gaeliran held his hands up, calling out to hold fire.

"I wish to speak! What are you doing here? This is a peaceful station! You are infringing upon our neutrality rights!"

Gizan lifted his weapon and shot the man in the face. The body dropped to the floor and he continued moving, stepping over the corpse. The Pahxin and humans would not bother trying to surrender or talk. When they heard the weapons fire, they would be fully defensive. Unlike the fools on the shipyard station, these might be well trained.

I suspect this is where I will lose the majority of my people. Gizan already had to replace three men from the previous action and he intended to send the less skilled ahead as cannon fodder. Considering what they were facing and the stakes of the game, winning would be worth all their lives.

Another two Gaelirans attempted to talk to them and he gunned them down as well. This station will be coated in blood. Come to me, filth. I will cleanse you all.

***

☐
Chapter 6

Christina's ears twitched as she swore she heard a weapon fire. She drew her pistol and turned to Lothan. "Did you hear that? I think it came from outside our door."

He nodded his head. "Ambassador and aides ... please position yourselves under the table. It is for your safety."

Reach came close to Christina. "Do we have an extra gun?"

"Sir, while I'm certain you've shot someone before, I don't think risking you in a firefight is an option."

"I can help."

"We've got six people ready to do this." Christina looked him in the eyes. "I have to insist that you stay safe."

"I have no intention of cowering under a table!"

"Then don't cower," Christina replied. "Just keep out of the line of fire until we're done. We have the advantage in that they have to come to us. This doorway won't allow them to rush through easily. Providing they don't pop off some grenades, we should be fine and then we'll get back to the shuttle. For now ... I really need you to get to safety."

Reach scowled at her but complied, joining the other ambassadors. Christina let out a sigh of relief. Thank God. She tried to scan the area, to see if she could figure out what was coming for them but the jamming extended to all functions on her tablet. The bodyguards moved to either side of the door, weapons held high.

Christina stood just to the left and a few feet away, straining to hear more. Footsteps approached, coming rapidly. Another couple shots rang out, beam weapons that hummed and spit. Someone screamed. Something heavy hit the ground. Someone tried to open the door, the sounds of them violently tapping the panel quite clear.

Well, here they come. She cleared her throat. "We're not letting you in."

"Filthy human scum," a man's gruff voice replied. "We will skin you alive if you do not open this door immediately."

"Oh, well ... since you're so polite ..." Christina rolled her eyes. "On second thought, I've changed my mind. You're going to have to figure out how to get in here without our help."

They started shouting in Pahxin so rapidly and violently her computer couldn't keep up with the translation. She turned to Lothan who wore a grim expression. He shook his head at her and motioned to the door. "They have a computer expert who can open the door and while he works, they are looking for a key."

"Lovely. How long do you think it'll take?"

"Not very."

"Do you think we could make it to your shuttles?" Christina asked. "While they're fiddling with this door."

"It depends on how many there are," Lothan replied. "They have access to both sides of this conference room. However, if there are not very many, it may be worth the risk.

Christina thought back to their walk through the station to the conference room. The area had been pretty open with no cover to speak of. If they ran for it and were attacked, there wasn't anything to hide behind. A better tactic might have been to remain where they were and wait for backup. If only they could communicate

"I'm sure our people will send help," Christina said. "As soon as they notice what's going on."

"I completely agree." Lothan scowled. "I believe we should wait here … at least until such time that we must move."

"Alright, I guess we hold them here," Christina replied. Hurry up, Gnosis. I hope you noticed what's going on over here. We could really use some damn help.

***

Desmond grabbed his seat as the ship shook violently. One of the Tol'An destroyers scored a direct hit to the bow. Salina called out that the shields held but the impact caused minor concussion damage. Engineering would start gathering data on what they needed to repair.

"Zach, what happened to evasive maneuvers?" Vincent asked.

"Sorry, sir." Zach's hands moved over the controls in a blur. "Their targeting systems are absurd. We're engaged with one of the Pahxin military vessels…it's nothing like the ships we fought back on Earth or even when we encountered them at the other planet. These were built for professional combat."

"Cassie," Desmond said. "Can you jam their targeting? Buy us some room?"

"I'll try … I'm still waiting for the probe to get into position anyway."

"Return fire with everything we've got," Desmond ordered. "How are the fighters doing?"

"Holding their own," Vincent replied. "The one man Tol'An ships aren't as dangerous as the Kalrawv Group proved to be. Plus, the Pahxin have their own people out there partnering with us."

The ship vibrated almost imperceptibly as the weapons discharged. Every gun and beam weapon went off at the same time, sending out enough firepower to tear through an unshielded ship in seconds. A moment later, the engines kicked in and Zach initiated a quick maneuver to nudge them backward.

The extra range might mean some of their shots miss when they retaliate, Desmond thought. Good call.

"Several direct hits," Zach said. "They turned just before though and I got them on the Starboard side."

"Salina?" Vincent asked. "What are you reading?"

"Their shields on that side have dropped to forty percent," Salina replied. "They're dealing with some passthrough damage as well."

"They're turning again," Zach announced. "Yep … showing me their Port side now."

"I see what they're up to." Desmond leaned back. "Are we ready to fire again? If so, let's whittle down their shields on all fronts. Eventually, we'll have to overload them."

"They're retaliating." Zach worked the controls again and the ship lurched hard to starboard. Desmond was jostled in his seat but they didn't experience the same pounding as before. Still, something hit them causing a shimmer more than a heavy shake. He glanced at his own computer to see what came up.

"Shields seem to have taken the brunt of that one too," Desmond announced. "Do you have anything more specific? How dangerous was that hit, Salina?"

"It seems ..." Salina paused. "They were attacking the shields specifically. They're dropping in that section. Some kind of ... strange drain. It's lingering."

"What do you even mean?" Vincent asked. "What's lingering?"

"I see it," Cassie added. "We have to drop the shields in that area I think. Reboot them. Can we turn so they don't have a good shot on our weakened side?"

Zach fired the weapons again.

"That might not have been a good idea," Salina said. "The power drain from our beam weapons dropped those shields further. They're at twenty percent and if they drop to zero, it will likely overload the generators. I might not be able to get them back online without extensive repairs."

"Turn us," Desmond said. "Put our good side to them and Salina, get those shields back up. I don't care what it takes."

Zach initiated the maneuver. "I hit them," he added, "solid blow to the other side. Looks like the shields held better there though. They might've reinforced them."

"Very likely," Cassie said. "I think—"

Before she could finish her sentence the ship shook violently and the lights dimmed. Desmond spun toward Salina. "What the hell was that?"

"Looks like someone hit us with a missile...or even a bomb." Salina shook her head. "Extensive damage to decks seven and eight … crew quarters and one of the medical bays. Casualty reports are coming in."

"Was that a smaller ship that deployed the attack?" Desmond asked. "How'd they pull that off?"

"It must've been," Vincent replied. "I'll work with the fighters to flush that thing out."

"Good, get it out of here." Desmond shook his head. "Can we get the shields back online?"

"I'm working on it now, sir." Salina actually sounded frustrated, which surprised Desmond. He'd never heard her get annoyed before. "I'll know in a few moments."

"Do what you can … but hurry. We're not in a place where we can afford to take this slow."

***

Dennis's shields returned to full power and he redirected his ship back to the fight. Dala formed up beside him as they made their approach, her ship less than five hundred meters away—close enough to make out some of the details.

They operated with twin thrusters in the back and deployable wings on the sides. The cockpit was conical with the pilot occupying the top near the back. Dark gray panels covered the hull and the shields made the whole thing look slightly blurry. Weapons bristled on the bottom and sides, beam weapons by the look of them.

"Thanks for staying with me," Dennis said. "Do you need to return to your wing?"

"I'm with my assignment," Dala replied. "When we return to the fray, I'll make my way back to the others. For now, I think we need to get you back to your people, don't you think?"

Dennis wasn't going to argue. Mustang squadron was deep in the thick of battle, taking on dozens of Tol'An fighters. Their allies were winning the fight but that didn't mean the fanatics were slowing down. They continued to throw themselves into the brawl, seemingly oblivious to self-preservation.

Their ships aren't as good but they're proving to be more dangerous than the Kalrawv Group at this point.

"Mustang One, come in." Vincent's voice filled his cockpit. "Can you read me, over?"

"I read you," Dennis replied. "What's going on?"

"I see that you're not in the middle of the combat zone."

"Just taking care of some damage. I'm about to be back in it."

"Fall back," Vincent replied quickly. "I have an assignment for you so don't engage."

"Okay ... but I'm with one of the Pahxin fighters. She needs to get back to her wing, sir."

"If she's there, you might see if she'll back you up. We've got a ship out here harassing us with missiles. It's caused some pretty significant damage. You need to find him and take him out."

"Wow ... Okay, I'm on it." Dennis frowned. "I'll let Mustang know I'm not coming right back and head there now. Do you have a signature or anything?"

"It was last seen off the port side somewhere. Get over there and begin your investigation but I doubt it will be hard to find. It wants to finish us off, I promise you that."

"Okay, we're on it." Dennis switched over to Dala as he adjusted course for the Gnosis. "Change of plans. We have a ship causing some trouble over here. Want to come back me up while I get rid of him?"

"I can do so," Dala replied. "We can't afford you to lose your largest ship."

Dennis dropped a message to Shane letting him know what was happening and to continue the fight there. He would join them when he finished. If I pull this off and don't find a way to get shot down myself. God knows if this guy is capable of evading the automated defenses of the Gnosis, I might be in over my head.

Dala allowed him to take the lead, following close behind and to the right. He wondered about his situation, how he ended up with one of their new allies flying with him. Much as he hated to use the word, it felt like fate. They needed to learn to work together and perhaps the negotiating table wasn't the place to do so.

Out there, fighting the Tol'An, they came together like soldiers and when they finished, providing they won, they'd have a victory to share. As long as the politicians didn't turn it into a pissing contest, it might do more for Pahxin/human unity than all the conversations and gift giving in the universe.

The Gnosis became larger as they approached. A Tol'An destroyer engaged them, a slightly smaller ship in comparison to the human craft but quite deadly from the scans. Cannon fire from the Gnosis lit space up and they scored a solid hit on their target. Dennis frowned at the action.

Why didn't the Tol'An even try to evade that? They didn't so much as move.

"Did you see that?" Dennis asked Dala.

"Yes, this is looking more like a distraction every moment."

"A distraction?" Dennis hummed. "Not an attack?"

"Oh, they are attacking ... but why?" Dala clicked her tongue. "Their objective is not likely the destruction of our vessels but of our alliance. Depending on how they planned to go about that task, it may be quite the surprise. Of course, if I were willing to bet, I would say they have attacked the station as well and are trying to assassinate our ambassadors."

"That would be screwed up! I can't believe—" Dennis paused as his scanner picked up motion on extreme range up ahead, something small. "I think I've got our target. Did you pick anything up?"

"Negative," Dala said. "I'll follow your lead. Take us closer."

Dennis redirected his course and engaged the afterburners. The extra propulsion crammed him into his seat and he forced himself to relax into it. Inertial dampeners eventually caught up, alleviating the pressure. They only had to fly a few moments before the blip reappeared.

Dala chuckled over the line. "I've got it now. They think they're clever hovering around debris. It masks their signature but not completely. Hit and run ... Hide while the larger ship contends with the more immediate threat then dash out to take advantage of any damage done. It will be a fast ship with heavy weapons but limited defenses."

"So easy to take down, right?"

"Target locks will be ineffective so not easy." Dala paused. "Note that we've been detected and they know we're onto them."

Dennis checked the scanner and sure enough, the enemy ship was on the move, flying away from the Gnosis. The speed surprised him and he'd have to engage full throttle plus the afterburners to catch up. Both would put a drain on his beam weapons but at least the guns would be unaffected.

"We'd better hit it," Dennis said. "Though I'm not entirely sure where they think they're going."

"Their goal is to lure us away from the battle, removing two combat pieces from the engagement. If we ignore it and go back, it will simply continue harassing the Gnosis. The Tol'An fail to grasp the fact we have good reason to track this thing down and destroy it. If not for this fight, then the next one."

Dennis engaged his engines and hit the afterburners, shifting more power for additional speed. Once he was underway, he asked, "Is this ship their own design or something?"

"A modification on an old one," Dala replied. "They took our original fighters and threw out everything they didn't need, including life support. The person piloting that ship is wearing a full environmental suit and that limits the amount of time they can fly. They also lack the ejection thrusters required to save the person should the ship experience a problem."

"Jesus, that's insane!"

"I am not sure what you mean by that..."

Dennis cleared his throat. "Um ... nothing. Just ... slang I guess." They were closing on the target but not quickly. He checked their range and they were well away from the Gnosis, having traveled over five thousand kilometers. *At least we got this guy off their backs. First part of the plan accomplished. The next part seems like it'll be a lot more difficult.*

"Keep going straight," Dala said. "I'll see what I can do about driving him into an attack."

"Wait! How are you going to ..." Dennis paused as he watched Dala's ship dart off, leaving him behind as if he were standing still. "Catch ... up ... wow. You guys are fast."

"I'm sure when the talks are over, we'll share this information. For now ... be prepared to shoot."

The enemy turned sharply, banking hard to the left. Dala matched its motion, leading it and firing at extreme range. Purple lights flashed from her weapons, winking out as quickly as they appeared. Though they didn't seem to come anywhere near the target, it swung wildly around, flying away from her attack.

Dennis continued on his course, checking his distance to target. He figured he didn't even have a slim chance of scoring a hit at that range and so he remained patient, letting Dala do her work. She pushed her ship hard, the thrusters at the back burning bright. Cutting around, she fired again, this time at its rear.

This had the effect of speeding the enemy up and it began flying roughly in Dennis's direction. With it coming closer, the range rapidly became less of a problem. The targeting computer tried to snag a link but failed. Dennis did his best judgement call and pulled the trigger, then readjusted to fire again.

The first volley of projectiles were a clean miss but the second came close enough to make the enemy perform a barrel roll and dive. Dennis adjusted course to pursue just as Dala came up on its rear. She fired again and one side of her beam weapon hit. Shields flared and the enemy climbed, a tight maneuver that should've turned the pilot into paste.

Lord, their dampeners are incredible! Dennis pulled up as dramatically as he dared and he still felt extreme pressure from the G force. Leveling out, he was on target again but his heart skipped a beat when he noticed the enemy was coming straight for him. Rolling to the right, his ship took a blow from energy weapons on the bottom, searing his shields.

The generator issued a warning moments before it began the recharge process. *From one hundred percent down to fifty in one shot—and not even both beams. Dala wasn't kidding about how tough these things are. That was incredible!* He looked over his shoulder, noting the enemy didn't have a chance to come after him.

Dala fired relentlessly, forcing their opponent to go into a fully defensive mode. It swung around, moving like an angry bee but it couldn't shake the Pahxin pilot from its tail. Dennis veered around and tried to catch up with her, moving in low. He called his shot so she wouldn't fly in his path, blasting away at the enemy.

It took one of his rounds and rocketed off suddenly, as if it supercharged its engines. *There's no way the pilot handled that!* Dennis shook his head, staring with wide eyes. "What just happened?"

"He just used his advantage," Dala said. "And it won't save him for long. Whatever fuel he has left will be diminished. We can stay with him and catch up or return to the Gnosis. I do not believe he has enough to make it home or to cause any more trouble but … the assignment is yours. I will defer to your judgement."

Dennis checked the course heading for the enemy and frowned at what it was racing toward. A small asteroid field lay not even five hundred kilometers away. If it was going in there, it would be easier to hide. Maybe he thought he could call for some help and his buddies would come and save him later.

I don't want to leave him out here to cause more trouble later. "I think we should go after him. Make sure he's done."

"Then we shall." Dala altered course and gave chase. "Be mindful of the asteroids. His signature will be difficult to make out amongst them."

Yeah, I'm sure he's counting on that. "Got it ... Let's make it happen."

***

Gunnery Sergeant Geoff 'Heat' Heathrow boarded the shuttle in his power armor and took his customary seat near the pilot's seat. Seregeant Lawrence Gorman, Lieutenant Brent Fielding and Corporal Willis Anderson rounded out the four man team going to help the ambassadors. They decided any additional manpower would be overkill in the tight quarters.

Fielding was new to the team, having only joined the Gnosis a day before they departed. He barely had a chance to speak to the men or let them know his expectations before they were thrown into a mission with him. All Heat knew about the man came from stories of his field service. Apparently, the guy was pretty tough.

They expected more time to acclimate to him, that they were going on a milk run where they could chat and get to know their new team lead. Instead, they had to find out what he was made of in conflict, not exactly the best place to build trust. Still, he picked the men with confidence and was the first one to say he'd be right there with them.

I already like him better than our last guy ... This one seems to know what he's doing. I'm not afraid we're going to be led astray.

"We'll be there in about three minutes," Warrant Officer Jeb Douglas announced. He was one of the most daring and crazy pilots in the crew and bringing him along meant they would certainly arrive swiftly but not necessarily safely. "I'm going to recommend everyone strap in for this though. We're going to be hauling some serious ass."

"Thank you," Fielding replied. "I've heard stories about this guy and I'm assuming all of you are quite familiar. We're going in near the Pahxin shuttles as it's closer to the Gnosis. I'm thinking there's a possibility that we're going to be shooting right away so be prepared for that eventuality. HUD check in flight. Let's fall out, Mister Douglas."

The shuttle launched without preamble and the moment they cleared the deck, Jeb hit the thrusters and propelled them out. Afterburners kicked in and the ship hurtled toward the station at a rapid pace. Heat looked out the window, noting how quickly their destination was growing.

A destroyer engaged the Gnosis, exchanging blasts as the two capital ships lumbered in various directions, attempting to mitigate the damage as it came in. Fighters buzzed one another in the opposite direction, engaged in a flurry of combat. A massive Tol'An battleship duked it out with the Pahxin capital vessels.

The sheer chaos in the area must've been particularly painful for the Gaelirans to behold, considering their neutral status. But just then, the humans and Pahxin were working to keep them all safe. Hopefully, they'd be grateful or at least not angry. Clearly, the negotiations brought the trouble.

Were their hosts the type to hold grudges?

Probably not, Heat mused. Someone must've brought this kind of nonsense to their door before. You don't offer a place for peace without the occasional flared temper.

"Two minutes to contact," Jeb said. "Communications are iffy so you're going to need to find a way in when I get us linked up with the door I've found."

"Maybe the internal coms are working," Gorman offered. "When we get close, we should be able to open the outer door easily enough then com someone for the inner door."

"Let's plan to open them both ourselves," Fielding said. "We can't be sure of any assistance on there and if we have to, we might need to blow that door and use our own pressurization to keep from killing everyone on board."

That sounds extreme, Heat thought. *But then again, we are talking about a desperate situation. The Tol'An might blow up the entire station. We can only speculate why they're really here.*

"Coming in hot," Jeb said. "Hold on, everyone! This is going to be interesting."

"I hate when you say that," Heat called out, gripping his seat tightly. "It always proves to be too accurate."

***

Christina's ears rang as total chaos erupted around her. She shoved herself up from the ground and fired her weapon at the smoking remains of the door, three shots disappearing into the smog. People shouted around her, screams of pain and she crawled her way to the table where the VIPs were still located.

Admiral Reach was still moving as was the ambassador for the Pahxin. Bodyguards from both sides engaged in combat, first with firearms but they were forced into a wild melee. Christina realized the time for waiting was over. They couldn't hold the enemy there. It was time to move.

"We have to go!" Christina shouted. "Admiral, you have to follow me. Now!"

"What about the bodyguards?" Reach shouted. "Shouldn't they be controlling this?"

Christina cursed under her breath. "I'm AIA, sir. I'm sorry to bring this to your attention now but we don't have time for arguing. If we want to get out of this alive, you're going to have to trust me. Come on. Now!"

She pulled his arm and they left the table, moving for the opposite door that had just been destroyed. Reach crouched as they moved and he opened the door while Christina fired suppressive shots at the doorway. Lothan arrived with his ambassador, prepared to make a run for it as well.

"When this opens," Christina said, "we're going to have to take the lead. Chances are good we're about to encounter enemies out there."

"I agree." Lothan grunted. "I'll take the lead, you follow the rear and ensure no one lags behind. I know the way to our shuttle."

"Okay ..." Christina turned to Reach. "Stay in the middle and remain close to the other ambassador. When that door opens, follow Lothan no matter what. Ready?" The door slid aside, revealing the open space between the conference room and the nearest hallway some sixty feet away. "Go! Go! Go!"

The four of them darted from the room, leaving the bodyguards to hold the Tol'An back. Gunfire continued blasting back there but at least immediately, the small VIP party was not pursued. Christina kept her head on a swivel, keeping an eye on the two hallways which might admit attackers.

One came running from the left and Christina whipped off a snap shot, catching him in the throat. He fell to the ground, grasping at the wound as he convulsed his way toward death. The next one must've seen his friend go down because he didn't come out but rather used the corner for cover and fired at them.

Okay, so they aren't trying to catch us, Christina thought, ducking her head. "I suggest we sprint, everyone!"

The others picked up the pace and Christina returned fire again, this time lighting up the wall near their attacker. Just then another man rounded the other corner and started shouting at them. She couldn't make out what he had to say nor was her computer able to translate on the fly but it didn't sound pleasant.

Either he's saying die horribly or surrender. The Pahxin aren't stopping so I'm not going to either.

They made the entrance to the hallway and poured in with Christina hesitating just inside to see how bad it was. Where are the bodyguards? Come on, guys! Please tell me you made it! The coms were still down internally and she cursed as she caught up with the others. They were nearly thirty feet away when she started running.

An explosion rocked the station and Christina stumbled into the wall. Catching her balance, she shouted at her companions, "you don't think they're shelling the station, do you?"

"I would not put it past them!" Lothan cried back. "They've been known to be so thorough before … even with their own people aboard."

"Fantastic!" Christina shook her head, watching behind them carefully in the event they were being pursued.

They emerged into another room and Lothan stopped them abruptly. "Hold!" He shouted. "We are in trouble."

"What's wrong?" Christina asked the question but when she followed his gaze, she didn't need the answer. The Pahxin shuttle had been destroyed, torn free from its docking clamp. The inner door held but the outer was gone. If it had caused any more damage, they would all be dead. "Our shuttle is in the hangar … not docked like this. We can make it there."

"We should definitely try," Lothan said. "And we don't have to go back the way we came. We can go around down that maintenance corridor there!"

"How do you know?" Christina grabbed his arm. "We could get trapped in there."

"He seems pretty confident," Reach said. "And we don't have time for debate."

"I've been here many times and studied the layout extensively," Lothan explained, "not just the map they provided but one we were able to fashion ourselves through extensive visits and tours. Trust me, we can get where we're going through there but we have to hurry. Undoubtedly, our enemies will follow us."

"Okay, lead the way." Christina didn't like it but the admiral was right. They didn't really have a choice. *I hope Lothan knows what he's doing. If we get trapped down there, we're just going to die tired.*

☐

Chapter 7

A bright flash off to the starboard made Desmond's heart thump harder in his chest. It lingered for a good half minute before burning out. The destroyer was falling back just as they were, giving each ship a little room in the continuing struggle. Both ships had taken some damage but defenses kept them from experiencing any real operational impact.

"What was that?" Vincent asked.

"One of the Pahxin ships," Salina said. "It's … been destroyed."

"That battleship?" Desmond asked. "That thing looked tough."

"Yes, sir." Salina sighed. "And one of the other ships has taken significant damage. The remaining two are … undamaged so far."

Desmond turned to Vincent, "how're the fighters doing?"

"We've had no real casualties, just some damage. The Pahxin are tearing it up out there but they've lost six ships. Their tactics are ... daring to say the least."

"I can imagine." Desmond shook his head. "Cassie, where are we at with jamming their targeting?"

"I'm ready ..." Cassie tapped her screen a few times. "Now. Initiating a sensor blast."

The hull seemed to vibrate from whatever she did, not like when they fired their weapons. This was more subtle, something that Desmond only noticed due to his overwhelming familiarity with the Gnosis. "How will we know it worked?" He asked. "Maybe we need to just keep up with the evasive maneuvers?"

"I'll be able to tell momentarily," Cassie replied. "Also ... I'm blasting the probe now so we can try to communicate with the station. It might not work for long. Actually ... neither of the things I tried will likely last but if either do, we'll have a brief advantage. Initiating the other jamming signal now."

Salina went to work on her station, trying to hail the admiral's party. Desmond directed Zach to keep the pressure on the destroyer. Weapons hammered the destroyer again, and it picked up the pace as it moved away. *Is he actually falling back because he's concerned about us or are we being drawn into an attack?*

"Cassie, I really need an update on whether your jamming thing worked …" Desmond tapped the arm of his chair. "Pretty much now."

***

Cassie's eyes flew over the readings on her screen and she grunted in frustration. "My scans aren't coming back as fast as I'd like. There's a ton of interference in this sector, not just from what we've done but the enemy as well. Everyone's trying to talk to one another … It's a real mess out there."

"Just do whatever it takes," Desmond replied. "And hurry."

Like I'm not hurrying! Cassie kept her frustration to herself and continued typing as quickly as she could. Salina hailed the station, asking them in her calm voice to respond. Cassie's probe scheme might not have been powerful enough to prevent the other ship from blocking their communications, which would round out another failure.

I feel like I need some kind of practice at this point! Cassie clenched her fists and nearly started cursing out loud when her scan data finally came back. Thank God! What happened?

The destroyer was experiencing a variety of system failures, not just from her jamming signal but from damage as well. She reported this to Desmond immediately, stating that one of their attacks impacted their shield generators. They still had several but they were under the strain of having to compensate for the broken one.

"Don't let up," Desmond said to Zach. "I want you to time our shots so you are constantly hitting them. We no longer have to punch through the defenses, we just have to wear them down."

"Got it," Zach acknowledged while typing away, presumably programming the attack protocol.

Cassie leaned over to Salina. "Is it the same static you were getting before?"

"No, I believe I'm getting through now," Salina replied. "But they aren't picking up. The line's mostly clear. Not even the admins are answering though. I hope they're all just busy and not … well … dead."

Cassie's terminal began to beep. A message was coming through a private, encrypted channel. She put her earpiece in and spoke softly. "Hello? I'm here."

"Cassandra!" Christina's voice was colored with static. "I don't know how you all punched through the interference, but good job. We're in a lot of trouble down here. Our bodyguards are very likely dead and we're being pursued. Right now, we're in a maintenance passage heading back toward the hangar."

"Is the admiral okay?" Cassie asked. "The Pahxin ambassador?"

"They're fine and with me now. The Pahxin shuttle was docked, not at the hangar but attached outside. It's been destroyed. I don't know exactly how many enemies we're dealing with here but they've caused some serious havoc throughout the ship. Do you have an accurate count?"

Cassie frowned. "Negative, we're unable to scan the station right now, even with the jamming signal down. I do have some good news. We have marines incoming. If you can rendezvous with them, they should be able to get you out of there."

"Perfect. We'll try to coordinate with them upon arrival. How long before they are here and how much more time do we have with this com signal before it's down?"

"Oh boy …" Cassie looked over her screen for inspiration but there was no way of knowing for sure. "I can't say. I've got a probe producing interference near the enemy ship that caused our coms to go down. If it runs out of power, gets destroyed or they figure out how to compensate … not long."

"Understood. Let's maintain contact for as long as possible. In fact, can you patch me through to the marines? I can give them a general idea of where we're at."

"I'm on it." Cassie brought the marine lieutenant on the line. "Lieutenant Fielding, I've got Major Dawson on com. Can you coordinate quickly before we lose coms again? You might not have another chance."

"We'll make arrangements," Fielding replied. "Give us a rundown of where you're at, Major."

The conversation progressed and Cassie turned her attention to the battle raging outside. Nothing shook for the past few moments so they must not have taken a direct hit. Zach fired the weapons, scoring a hit on the side of the destroyer. Something sparked on the enemy hull, a quick flash that faded in an instant.

"One of their engines has shorted out," Salina announced. "Their generators are overloading. Shields are likely down but ... that isn't stopping them from moving. They're advancing on us now. Speed increasing."

"Take us up while you fire," Desmond said. "Make sure they can't ram us ... if that's what they really intend to do."

Their weapons blasted the surface of the ship, plowing into the unshielded bow. Chunks of metal flew clear and electrical pulses danced over the surface. They lost directional control and began to tumble. Zach hit the thrusters and pulled them well away as the enemy ship exploded in a brilliant purple glow that winked out in an instant.

Desmond slapped his knee. "Excellent job. We need a full damage report. What else is going on out there?"

"The enemy battleship is moving away," Salina replied. "The Pahxin have taken out the other destroyer. The scouts are still causing some trouble though and I'm not sure what that tech ship is doing. It remains out of range...but our forces are closing on it."

"Fighters have the field under control," Vincent added. "The enemy fighters are down to less than twenty percent of their starting forces...yet they aren't giving up either. We've got multiple ships damaged but not have been total losses."

"Much better than the fight with the Kalrawv Group." Desmond turned to Salina. "Get Ulian on the line. I want to talk about mopping this up … and figure out what exactly is happening on the station."

***

Squadron Leader Anna Jager found herself lost in the trance of combat, a state she wondered if she'd ever get to again after being shot down during the last mission. Her lack of fear surprised her and she settled back into the fighter with the same calm she always did. The first fighter that buzzed her made her chest tingle but that was the extent of her concern.

Since the moment they entered the fray, she and the others dished out considerable damage to the enemy. Her own kill count tallied six but she paid the price for it with some serious shield damage and a generator that would need to be tweaked. All systems were functioning but they were not in an ideal state.

Anna watched one of the enemy ships acquire a decent firing solution on one of Mustang's fighters and she rushed to intercept, dodging debris and other vessels along the way. As she prepared to open fire, her ally suddenly spun in place, firing two shots that caught the pursuing target right in the nose.

The enemy began to spin and collided with a chunk of hull from another downed ship.

"Thanks for the attempted assist," Flying Officer Alicia Quinn replied. "I had him though."

Anna remembered her from the previous mission. She was one of the pilots who could definitely hold her own but usually at the expense of wild maneuvers bordering on flat out dangerous. They formed up together and redirected their course back toward a larger group of enemies.

"That was some move," Anna said. "Did the dampeners even help?"

"Not really," Alicia replied. "You have to not mind a little discomfort, that's all. Whoa!"

Alicia climbed suddenly as an enemy nearly collided with her. They seemed to be out of control and smoke poured out of one of their engines. Anna fired her weapons at a target directly in front of her, catching them on the side. The shields held but the blow made them dash off, flying away with full afterburners.

"You okay?" Anna asked. "We seem to be driving them back."

"I'm good," Alicia said. "And their battleship is really hauling ass. Maybe they want to get back to it before they're left here."

Another fighter took a potshot at Anna as it flew by but it felt more like it was simply harassing her than trying to cause real damage. She considered pursuing but a proximity alarm went off, indicating an impending collision to the left.

Anna banked hard to the right and hit the burners, narrowly avoiding a missile that had been intent to take her down. She climbed, dragging the projectile with her as it continued hot on her tail. The nearest large vessel was one of the enemy scouts but it was a good thirty seconds away at full burn.

It shouldn't have significant small fighter defenses. Let's try this.

Anna hurdled herself for the new target and Alicia caught up.

"Um ... what're you doing?" Alicia asked.

"Taking this missile for a spin."

"And people say I'm crazy." Alicia hummed. "I'll screen for you. There might be some obstacles ... like that one!" Something exploded in front of Anna and the pieces of it sizzled on her shields.

"What the hell was that?"

"Small rock. No big deal. But you didn't want to hit it."

"Thanks ..." Anna glanced at her scanner, noting the missile was gaining on her. I need to make it compensate to buy some distance. "I need to maneuver a bit to shake this thing loose."

"I've got a better idea," Alicia said. "Stay your course."

Anna watched as Alicia dropped back and flew directly between her and the missile. The projectile broke off and followed the new target, buying Anna a moment to breathe. "You really are crazy! We're taking that thing to the scout ... Can you get it there or am I going to have to pull that foolishness off too?"

"Nah, I've got it," Alicia said. "Just watch my back. I think there are a couple fighters incoming."

Anna looked over her shoulder and caught sight of the incoming enemies. She dropped low and rolled in place, getting her on course to take a shot. As she climbed, coming in below them, her weapons discharged. Beams tore through the shields and guns ripped apart the hull. One of the two ships went up in a ball and was gone.

The other broke off from Alicia and came after Anna. They performed a dance, a seemingly choreographed dogfight that went on for a good twenty seconds. An explosion to the Anna's left stole her attention for a brief moment, a flash from near the scout. Anna's opponent fired a volley at her and she took half the attack on her left side.

Another alarm went off, this one indicating that the shield generator was struggling to keep the emitters running. The enemy flew past her and she veered hard, coming around behind him. Opening up with every weapon, the lights dimmed in the cockpit but his engines burst a moment later, his ship disintegrated.

"Good shooting," Alicia said. "Missiles gone ... didn't do much to the scout but at least it isn't chasing us anymore. Know who fired it?"

"I don't." Anna frowned at her damage report. "I'm in a little trouble."

"Let's move toward the Gnosis and the others," Alicia replied. "Maybe the automated repair will get you back up before the next little bout ... if there even is one."

Various enemy ships winked off the scanner as they were taken out. All through the theater of operation, the Pahxin and Gnosis fighters worked in tandem to finish off the enemy. Their base retreated and it seemed as if they were being driven back. It looked positive, even as Anna kept a nervous eye on her defenses.

Would be nice if we were done, Anna thought. I wonder if they've succeeded at whatever they were trying to do on the station. It would explain their sudden retreat but I really hope we drove them off before they did something nefarious.

***

Dennis plotted a path for the enemy they were pursuing and noted that if it continued on its present course, it would arrive at the station shortly. What would it possibly want to do there? Why wouldn't it try to make it back to its battleship to get out of here? He checked the com traffic but it was still iffy with all the interference.

Still, messages were making it around the area and apparently, the marines were on their way to save the VIPs. That would make a good target. Stop the reinforcements from helping out. He tried to get a message to the shuttle but they were too far away. If only the noise levels weren't so high from all the activity …

A thought occurred to him. "Dala, can you get a message over to the station?"

"Negative, I am dealing with considerable interference." She paused. "And I see why you are concerned with that. Our target is probably going to harass the others. Perhaps even attack the hangar. Let us beat him to that location, shall we?"

Dala hit her afterburners and tore off, leaving Dennis as if he were standing still. He increased speed, pushing until he started to feel sick. Even then, he was only barely keeping up with her. *At least I'm still on her tail ... sort of. We really need to collaborate to get some of this technology in our ships.*

They flew for a good two minutes at the breakneck speed before he received a com message. *We must be close enough for the Gnosis to get us messages again.* Dennis dialed in the signal, working at it until the static dissipated. It sounded like someone was trying to communicate with the various pilots.

"Enemy is in retreat," Commander Bowman said. "This is a general recall for all pilots to return to the Gnosis. Repeat, return to base immediately. Over."

Dennis tapped to reply, "Commander, this is Arden. I'm afraid I'm still in the thick of something. That ship we've been chasing is heading for the station and we're thinking they plan to harass the shuttle. I'll return when it's done."

A brief, static pause sounded before Bowman replied. "Affirmative and understood. Do what you have to do then get back here. We might have to leave in a hurry."

Dennis lost connection to the Gnosis but he spoke to Dala. "Looks like we've got a deadline."

"We always did," Dala replied. "I am closing in but so are they. This will be close. Prepare to fire. Distracting him will be a good idea."

Dennis noted they were within what was considered long range. He fired a couple beam shots but they didn't come close. He still couldn't get good targeting on the bastard. Dala tried as well but they were both still too far out. The station loomed ahead and the enemy would have a chance to take some shots.

How close is the marine shuttle? Dennis checked the scanner and noted they were already attached to the station. They'll be inside in a moment but they'll still need a way out. Dala fired again, this time making the enemy climb, pushing him out of his attack run so he had to climb. It would take him a moment to return to his attack.

But instead of making for another angle, he came straight toward Dennis. Oh crap! Dennis hit the top thrusters, dropping down abruptly as a series of energy blasts went over him. Dala screamed by, trying to find a firing solution but the enemy was too swift. He made a quick loop and came at Dennis again, blasting him in the side.

The shields held but something sparked behind him. Navigation gave him an error but he didn't mind as much about that. As long as he still had weapons and some defenses, he'd be fine. Performing a barrel roll, he pulled up sharply and came around, avoiding another attack while putting himself in a better position to retaliate.

They entered a dogfight, veering around one another but it was clear that Dennis couldn't out maneuver his opponent. He needed to distract him, to give his impromptu wingmate a chance to take a shot.

"Pull up hard now!" Dala yelled. "Now!"

Dennis complied immediately, gritting his teeth at the sudden G force. His opponent flew by behind him and Dala swooped in, weapons firing in rapid volleys. As Dennis leveled out, he saw them take the brunt of most of the attacks, tearing through their defenses.

Fire billowed from the enemy's engines in great orange blobs but he still managed to spin and take a shot at Dala. She performed an evasive maneuver but still took the brunt of the attack, sheering off a large chunk of her ship on the side. The enemy exploded even as she began to tumble.

"Dala! Do you have to eject?" She didn't immediately reply and he tried again. "Can you hear me?"

"I can hear you, human," Dala replied through gritted teeth. I am in the middle of getting this thing under control. Do not worry. I should not have to abandon this vessel though it will require considerable repairs."

"If you can joke, you must be fine." Dennis relaxed into his seat as she regained control. "Come on, I'll escort you back ... The smoke coming out of your side there doesn't look good."

"Thank you." Dala adjusted her course, heading toward the other Pahxin ships.

Dennis couldn't help but feel as if the fight they'd just finished might've been too easy, too simple. Having finished it, only one ship against two did seem ridiculous but the specialization of the technology, the speed and inability to be targeted made it far more dangerous than the rank and file ships they encountered.

"I appreciate your help, Dala. I mean it, I couldn't have done this without you."

"Cooperation is what we are meant to do," Dala replied. "I am simply glad we were able to work together effectively. Perhaps we will see each other again when this is all over with."

"Definitely." Dennis drew a deep breath and continued on in silence. His part of the fight was done, at least for the moment.

***

Christina continued to hold their flank as they made their way through the narrow corridor of the maintenance tunnel. She spoke briefly with the marines and sent her position to them. They committed to meeting them where they might emerge, taking care of any of the Tol'An they came across.

"Backup is here," Christina announced. "Our marines are making their way through the station now and they're going to meet us ASAP."

"Great news," Reach muttered. "How much longer are we going to be in this space?"

Aesthetics mattered to the rest of the station but the maintenance area was filthy by comparison. It was also several degrees hotter. Sweat made Christina's shirt cling to her skin and her hair became a matted mess plastered to her scalp. The others looked just as miserable, especially the Pahxin ambassador.

His clothes appeared to be heavy and they definitely weren't doing his mobility any favors.

"We're coming up on the panel to get out of here," Lothan said. "Stay close so I can scout the area. I want to ensure we have a safe path to the hangar."

"I'll hold them here," Christina said. *To the best of my ability.* The bodyguards carried heavier weapons than she did but the tunnel was narrow enough that the enemy shouldn't have been able to field more than two people at a time. She felt confident she could handle them for a while and, if necessary, the admiral was itching for a fight too.

The Pahxin ambassador won't be able to assist us. He was a true VIP that needed protection. If Lothan didn't return, he'd become Christina's responsibility and she needed to ensure he survived at all costs. Having him die in her custody would have tragic repercussions for their burgeoning alliance.

Lothan dislodged a panel in the wall and turned to them. "Be silent now ... I will return shortly."

He slipped outside and moved down the hallway, leaving them alone. Christina began to second guess the plan, wondering if they should've simply stayed together. Remaining in the maintenance passage felt foolish. Yes, the tight quarters might nullify the enemy's numbers but a lack of maneuverability went both ways.

"We have to go," Christina said. "We can't wait for Lothan."

"What?" Reach scowled. "I thought we were trusting him with this one."

"We're trapped in here ... We need room to move. I think—"

"Greetings," a low voice from behind interrupted Christina and she spun in place, preparing her weapon. A hard blow caught her wrist and her fingers reflexively opened. Her gun bounced off the wall but she didn't even spare it a look, instead throwing a kick at the person who attacked her.

He blocked the blow and they began a brutal melee. Christina threw a punch at the dark figures face, he deflected it and retaliated with a low kick. She danced back and bumped into the wall, using it to propel herself forward. She connected with his chest and followed with an upper cut.

The attack didn't land before she was shoved back and he clicked his tongue. "You might want to settle down, little human." Christina paused and glanced over her shoulder. Two men held guns on the ambassador and the admiral. "You don't want to lose your precious cargo, do you?"

Christina weighed her options. Would these fanatics kill them anyway? Reports suggested it was a distinct possibility. Where the hell are you, Lothan? She cursed under her breath but didn't lower her guard. Think! There has to be a way out of this! The admiral grunted as he was poked by one of the guns.

"I think we've lost this round, Major," Reach said. "Better to live through this to fight another day."

If we live. Christina straightened up. Her gut burned. "You win." The two words frustrated her and her face showed it. She scowled as the man gestured in her direction. Another of his men approached.

"Bind their hands and let's get them out of here. I'm impressed by the wily escape attempt but you never had a chance." He patted her on the shoulder. "You'll have the opportunity to understand why soon enough. Bring them. We must get to the ship and leave this forsaken place behind."

***

Heat took point, checking the corridor before dashing out and hurrying toward the conference room where the VIPs were. He passed by dozens of bodies, unarmed people in civilian garb. Some were shot, others cut open and blood soaked into the once nice carpet. Whoever went through there indulged some serious butchery.

"We're coming upon their last known location," Heat said. "You say they're in the maintenance corridors?"

"Yes," Fielding replied. "My HUD's acting up but I think I see a few panels to get in there. Our armor won't fit so we need to figure out where they're going to come through."

The door to the conference room was little more than debris. Heat and Gorman stepped inside and cleared the room, pausing when they came upon the corpses of the human bodyguards. One had been shot but the other ... Someone cut off his arms and his head lulled back, nearly severed.

"Jesus Christ ..." Gorman muttered. "Monstrous ..."

Heat grunted and looked around. "The fighting here was over fast. There aren't that many scorch marks on the wall. Hardly any missed shots." He noted one Tol'An soldier's body. "They only took one with them, too."

"And the animals left their own behind," Gorman said. "What's next?"

"Find the VIPs," Fielding replied. "Let's head back toward the hangar and see if we can't rendezvous with them. God knows how many more of these fanatics there are out there so stay sharp. I'm guessing we'll be in a firefight sooner than later."

They headed back down the hallway, past where their shuttle was located. Someone shouted up ahead, a loud woman's voice. "Can you hear me?"

"That was definitely English," Anderson said. "Must be one of ours!"

"Double time it!" Fielding ordered. "Spread out, Anderson and Gorman on our flanks. Heat, take my left."

Heat rushed down the hall, their armored boots hammering the floor. As they approached, there wouldn't be any stealth. Whatever fight was about to happen would be inevitable. The trick would be differentiating the friendlies from the enemies. If they were in close quarters, the marines needed to be precise with their shooting.

Rounding a curve, Fielding stopped abruptly. "Contact!" He fired his weapon and Heat moved closer to see what he was shooting at. There was a group of people approaching an airlock leading to another ship. Heat's HUD identified the various targets. Three friendlies and five Tol'An.

He took aim but paused. They were clustering up, forcing the VIPs into the shuttle. Firing their weapons risked hurting the people they were trying to save. "We have to find a way to keep that ship here!" He shouted, dropping low to clip one of the Tol'An in the leg. His target hit the ground and returned fire but he was rewarded with a head shot from Gorman.

"Gnosis!" Fielding shouted into the com. "Can you lock down the magnetics on the station to keep this ship here? They have the friendlies and are attempting to depart! We need immediate assistance!" Static filled the speakers. "Damn it, they must've lost com again! Gorman, what can you do?"

"Nothing from here!" Gorman replied. "I'd need to be at the control center and even then, this is alien tech. I'm not sure I'd be able to do much on short notice!"

"Let's get on board!" Anderson called. "If we're on there, they can't exactly leave."

"No." Fielding shook his head. The rest of the Tol'An boarded the ship. "They've gotten away. We need them to be disabled out there to take them back."

"We have another problem." The voice came from behind them and the marines spun in place, aiming at him. The Pahxin lifted his arms. "Please, don't shoot! I am Lothan! Bodyguard to the Pahxin ambassador! I'm on your side!"

"Why aren't you with them?" Fielding motioned with his head back toward the airlock which had closed up. "How'd you escape?"

"I was checking the way forward and had no idea that our enemies followed us through the maintenance tunnel." Lothan shook his head. "And while I was away, I found that they have trapped this station with explosives. We must disarm them!"

"Perfect." Fielding sighed. "I hope you know where they are."

"Engineering," Lothan replied. "And I can lead you there."

"We need coms, too." Fielding sighed as they began to move through the station. "Lots of work left to do, gentlemen. Don't slow down because the primary objective went south. We'll get them back. It'll just take a little longer than we anticipated, that's all."

☐

Chapter 8

Desmond watched the screen as the enemy began to depart. They lost their scout vessels and one of the destroyers. The battleship was quite a ways off, pressed by the three remaining Pahxin ships. The fourth remained behind to contend with heavy damage. As the fighters began returning to the ship, they took stock of their own casualties.

"We're conducting repairs," Salina said, "but the generators took quite the beating. Several crew quarters are not habitable and won't be for a while. One of the medical bays is totally offline and this has put a strain on the remaining space. We have twenty-five wounded and … I'm sorry to say, three dead."

"Thank you," Desmond replied. "Are we able to use the hyperdrive?"

"Chief Engineer Webber stated that we can enter hyperspace if necessary." Salina hesitated before going on. "Sorry, I just got a report from engineering. They've deployed crews throughout the ship and are beginning various repairs. They estimate the generators will be in regular operating condition within half an hour. The rest … will take longer."

Ulian appeared on the screen suddenly enough to startle Desmond out of what he was going to say. "Um … hello."

"Captain," Ulian began. "It seems the ambassadors have been taken. They are in a fast assault shuttle rapidly departing the area. Check your scans as we have sent you the signature."

Salina complied and a smaller screen appeared beside Ulian's head. It showed a blip flying quickly away from the station but it was hard to maintain the readings. So they were here to kidnap people. What the hell happened to the marines? Looks like we're not done with this mission after all.

"We'll need to get our people back aboard and pursue," Desmond replied. "Do we know where they are going?"

"Not yet," Ulian said. "But our ambassador has a tracking device." He paused and uttered something that the computer would not translate. "It appears one of our vessels has just shot the escaping vessel. It has been damaged but not enough to stop it from leaving the system. Perhaps they won't go as far now."

Desmond frowned. "That was risky. Your people could've taken them out."

"Yes, I recognize this. We have another problem, as if the current situation is not trying enough. We have learned there are bombs planted on the space station. Your people are contending with them now. Providing they are swift, we should be able to depart the moment we know where the ambassador has stopped."

"You can track them from so far?" Desmond asked.

"Yes."

Direct, Desmond thought. "Okay, coms must be restored so we'll coordinate with our people on the station, get them back and come with you. Thank you for the heads-up." He watched as the remaining Tol'An ships dropped into hyperspace. *I wonder if we'll be dealing with that battleship after all.*

"You fought well today, captain. Forgive my reluctance and lack of faith. You and your people have proven yourselves capable. Ulian out."

"Er ... yay?" Vincent offered. "At least they're impressed?"

"That's something." Desmond stood up. "Let's make sure we focus our repair efforts on defense and departure. Get the marines on coms and help if they need it. Sounds like the bombs aren't too big of a deal or Ulian might've had an expression. Depending on how long we have to wait, we might be in for quite the trip."

***

Seven Hours Later

Desmond sat in the briefing room nearly, going through various reports. The Gaelirans issued a formal declaration of their appreciation to both the Gnosis crew and the Pahxin ships for helping with the Tol'An. Gorman and Lothan were able to disarm the bombs and properly dispose of them, so that alone ingratiated them to the inhabitants.

Admiral Reach's bodyguards were returned to the Gnosis and properly stored so they could be interred back home. The report suggested the marines were pretty unhappy about it, especially considering one of the two men had been badly brutalized. Captain Gabriel committed to having a meeting with them in an effort to calm them down.

Chief Engineer Webber made it clear that the repairs were going well. They were inside safety margins for a hyperspace run. Ulian sent a message along that stated they knew where the Tol'An had stopped and so they'd be leaving soon. The few other small problems they needed to work out could wait until they got home.

Desmond sent a communication request to the Pahxin. He needed to speak to Ulian about their course of action and how they intended to conduct the next part of the operation. When the commander's face appeared on the screen, Desmond dove right in, having learned his counterpart preferred to simply get to the point.

"I'd like a better understanding what the plan is for attacking the Tol'An."

Ulian nodded. "I understand. We will likely find an outpost there, a launching point for terrorist operations. My proposal is we go into the area ready for battle. We will deploy fighters, bombers and soldiers to secure the area and the hostages. My navigator will work with yours so you can arrive much closer to the target."

"Sounds good," Desmond replied. "How soon will we be able to go?"

"When we deliver the coordinates to you and have them fully plotted, we will depart. The Gaelirans have given us their blessing and they are ready to see us gone. They have many dead to put to rest and a station to clean up. We will speak again soon, Captain Bradford. Thank you for reaching out."

The screen went dark and Desmond sat back in his chair, feeling thoughtful. This next part of the assignment could be the most important. *A joint operation like this will see how we truly work together.*

The attack gave them a taste of unity but now they would be on the offense. Depending on what waited for them, they might find themselves in a tough spot. Four ships could probably take a small outpost but if it was some kind of main base with dozens of defenders, they'd be in for a real mess.

The Tol'An could not be allowed to keep the ambassadors regardless and waiting wasn't an option. The time to strike was upon them and as Desmond prepared himself for the unknown, tension began to build in his neck. Launching into a system without intel may have been required but it did not settle well for him as he considered all the lives about to be at risk.

***

Vincent checked in with the pilots thirty minutes before the ship was supposed to emerge from hyperspace. Engineering crews finished repairing the worst of the damage to the fighters and they were ready to go. The bombers were prepped and loaded. Three shuttles also idled, waiting for the marines to mount up.

Considering they had no idea what to expect, they were as prepared as they could be.

Vincent stopped at Cassie's quarters on his way to the bridge, knocking twice. Once they arrived at the station, they didn't have a chance to speak. Especially when the fighting started. Even when the enemy fled, they went in their own directions. She went to work with Thayne in regards to the signal the Tol'An used to selectively block communications.

The door opened and Cassie peered at him with wide eyes. She wasn't wearing her jacket yet and she buttoned the sleeves of her blouse. "Hey," she said, "what's up? Am I late?"

Vincent shook his head. "No, I just … I was heading to the bridge and thought you might be on that way too."

"Sure." Cassie grabbed her jacket and pulled it on, securing the buttons. "Let me grab my tablet and I'll be good to go."

They headed out into the hall a moment later, moving toward the elevator at a good clip. Vincent wasn't sure what to say. Platitudes seemed weak and he didn't want to make small talk, especially since he went out of his way to see her. He drew a deep breath and finally decided anything was better than nothing.

"How've you been? Has it been busy?"

"Oh, beyond," Cassie replied. "We made some headway into researching the weird signal they used to jam our coms. Thayne hadn't seen it before but it was definitely something from the Orbs. We don't know how to compensate for it yet but I think we can use a similar method to mute them when we arrive."

"Great news. I've been coordinating the marines and pilots. They're probably going to be busy." Vincent smirked. "What're the chances we show up and that ship is all alone? Wouldn't that be nice?"

"Impractical." Cassie returned his grin. "But hey, hope is important, right?"

The elevator arrived and they boarded. "When we get back, I trust you're going to throw yourself into research?"

"Depends on how fast we have to turn around and leave again," Cassie replied. "I wouldn't mind having a day off when we get back there. One that doesn't involve staying at Gamma Alpha."

"Seriously. I was wondering about that ..." Vincent cleared his throat. "Maybe we could break away for a few hours. Have lunch in the city at least."

Cassie nodded. "I'd like that. Maybe a commander will have a better chance to get us off the base than I typically do. I swear they think I'm some kind of extension of the Orb, like ... property."

"Your superiors?"

"And Harper," Cassie replied. "But especially the AIA. When I joined up, I thought it was just an amazing tech job but it consumes you fast. I'd like to say expectations are high but the reality is, they're exalted."

"What's the career path? Politics?"

"Advancement through the AIA, I guess." Cassie shrugged. "I got a promotion to senior agent when I got the assignment with the Gnosis. I'm not sure where I go from here but I suppose I'll find out soon enough."

The doors opened and the conversation ended. Captain Bradford stood at Zach's station and Salina chatted quietly on the com. Cassie sat at her console and Vincent logged into his own, checking for any new reports. The marines had boarded the shuttles and the fighter pilots signaled they were ready to go.

Okay, great news. Vincent leaned back in his seat, drawing a deep breath. He took a moment to relax. He might not get another for the next few hours. Considering the lives at stake and what it meant to humanity's plunge into the galactic theater, he felt the pressure resting on their success or failure.

Losing the ambassadors would transcend tragedy and represented a potential rift the two cultures might never mend. The thought should've filled Vincent with despair but instead, he found himself unusually calm. All things considered, worry wouldn't help his performance and the men under his command would certainly feel it.

***

Gizan fought to maintain discipline, to keep to his usual reserved nature. The situation on the station frustrated him. He lost five of his ten men and one of the humans proved to be more dangerous than he anticipated. Coupled with the fact that the ship was damaged on their way out of the system and he felt the mission could not have gone worse.

His navigator made it clear they could not make it back to the main base with their damage and adjusted on the fly. They had several safe planets throughout that region of space so it was just a matter of finding one close enough which could repair their damage. Gizan figured he could either interrogate the prisoners or commandeer another ship to get home.

At least the ships they lost were the ones he considered disposable. Unfortunately, they took several of their people with them. Recruits tended to be easy enough to come by but it would take time to replace them all. The Master might not be pleased with that aspect of what happened but when he had the prisoners in custody, he'd likely forget about it quickly enough.

Gizan wondered about the fallout from attacking the Gaelirans and killing so many of them. If the station blew up, things would be much more dramatic. Those neutral fools might even decry the Tol'An publicly, which in turn would enhance the organization's credibility. No one would doubt the conviction of Gizan's people again.

The human female proved to be of interest. Gizan wondered why she received such potent combat training. She seemed more capable than the two bodyguards they slaughtered and certainly more dangerous than the average Pahxin soldier. He looked forward to learning everything about her.

Tol'An interrogation methods involved acts which other cultures considered to be criminal in nature. Gizan believed the ends justified the means. If he got the information that he wanted, then he didn't care what he had to do to get it. He couldn't kill them but anything else was fair game.

After all, the Master planned to execute them publicly anyway. If they were battered up a little, perhaps missing a part, it wouldn't matter. They represented conviction more than anything. Humanity and the Pahxin would understand that the Tol'An were to be feared and respected.

"Sir," one of his soldier's interrupted his thoughts. "We have a concern about the human female."

Gizan sighed. "What?"

"We would've had to kill her if she didn't surrender. Would it be better to kill her now? Surely, we only need the ambassadors."

"For all we know, she is the proper ambassador." Gizan shook his head. "No, the only way these prisoners die is if the Master orders it."

"Yes, sir."

Gizan watched the screen as a timer ran down. It showed two and a half hours left before they would emerge from hyperspace. Plenty of time to reclaim his discipline, especially since he needed to send a message to the Master right away. Things were getting back on track. They simply needed a safe place to regroup.

***

Christina sat still beside Admiral Reach, her eyes closed. The metal bonds used by the Tol'An kept her hands close together, biting into her skin. She remained quiet, listening carefully to the ship noise around her. There were only seven people on board, including five soldiers, their leader and a pilot.

The craft was big enough to have a couple of rooms and the prisoners were kept in one of them but the voices of their captors carried. She listened to them speaking in their language, a mix between panic and unnerving calm. Half an hour into the trip, she labeled them in her head and started to prioritize them should the opportunity emerge to escape.

Hours later, the ship began to shake. Reach nudged her. "Major, are you awake?"

"Yes," Christina replied. "I have been this whole time."

"What was that? Do you know?"

"We've emerged from hyperspace."

"That didn't take long …"

"Seven hours, forty-three minutes," Christina said. "But you're correct, that was fast. Either their engines are more efficient than ours and they can cover greater distances faster or we haven't gone all that far."

"Which would you err on the side of?" Reach grunted. "Damn these cuffs!"

"We took a blow on our way out," Christina replied. "It caused some minor damage but it may have been enough to limit our options of where we could get to."

Reach sat quietly for a moment before speaking again, "I wonder why they haven't tried to interrogate us."

"No facilities." Christina opened her eyes and looked around. "This is a storage closet. They traveled light to grab us and get out. Now, wherever we end up … that's where they'll ask us questions. If they even bother. We're likely more useful as figurehead executions than anything else."

"Cheery thought, Major." Reach sighed. "So when did the AIA put you on me?"

"When I first joined your staff. Once it looked like the hyperspace drive would be successful, we wanted to be close to the military side of the program. Besides, having me around meant I could at least attempt to keep you safe. Had it not been for Lothan leaving us alone, we would've walked out of that maintenance tunnel."

"Do you think he's in on this?"

Christina shook her head. "No, I genuinely believe he thought he was doing the right thing. It just screwed us, that's all."

"We're not getting out of this … are we?"

"I intend to." Christina turned to him. "What about you?"

Reach's conviction returned, steadying his expression. He nodded once. "I do."

"Then we have to focus on that. There are always opportunities for escape. Believe me, prisoner transfers are never fully secure. Once they try to get us off this ship, we'll see what's possible…and exactly how we're going to get home."

***

Desmond felt his nerves bristle as they emerged from hyperspace. He figured he should've been used to it but each time, he had a moment of concern, however fleeting. The screens came on, showing they'd arrived within thirty-thousand kilometers from the planet—far closer than they would've without the help of the Pahxin navigator.

"Incredible," Zach said. "We hit our target within fifty kilometers."

"I've got enemy ships on scan," Salina said. "A destroyer, a scout, and two ships that ... I suppose the closest class to them would be the battleship from the previous sector but they have a different configuration. Also, there's a small facility on the planet. Working on number of inhabitants now."

"I'm jamming their communications," Cassie added. "They can't get a message out of the system to ask for help. Turnabout's fair play and all."

Ulian popped on their screen. "Captain Bradford. The ambassador has been taken to the planet's surface. That vessel we pursued was able to land. They have seventy-five individuals down there, not all of which will be combatants but that hardly matters. Our soldiers will have much work to do when we send them down."

Desmond scowled as he heard the news. "Understood. Our men are ready to go but we're going to need to escort them. That's some real opposition out there."

"Launch immediately. The enemy has yet to field their fighters and there are no ground defenses to take out our ships. When they've deployed, our soldiers will send you coordinates for landing. It's outside the facility but with your armor technology, you should be able to cover the ground quickly enough."

"Thanks," Desmond replied. "We're on it. What about the ships?"

Ulian smiled and it was not a pleasant look. "We destroy them all. Ulian out."

"Still charming," Vincent said as the screen went dark. "He's just not directing that ire at us."

"Disappointed?" Desmond asked.

Vincent shook his head. "Not at all."

"Deploy the shuttles and fighters," Desmond ordered. "Power up the weapons and defenses, Zach and move us into attack position. Time to get the admiral back."

***

Heat gripped his seat as the ship began to bounce. They'd entered the atmosphere but cloud coverage still blocked out details of the surface. Blue sky reminded the gunnery sergeant of home. Even so far from Earth, the look and feel of habitable planets were similar enough to not be a coincidence.

Perhaps that old species really did prepare these places for life, giving us all a chance to thrive.

The placid thought was quickly replaced by the briefing of the mission ahead. They were conducting a joint operation with the Pahxin soldiers to take a small facility. Intel was sparse. Scans gave them the size of the facility but not the internal layout. Some assumptions were made based on basic tactics.

A barracks was expected to be near the front gate. Short walls must've been erected to keep out wild life because they weren't tall enough to stop an invading force. The Pahxin suggested that the facility likely existed before the Tol'An occupied it, built by settlers long since departed.

They would land half a mile from their target then use their jump packs to get inside the perimeter. The VIP parties should've been easy to spot but they'd likely be in some kind of holding cells. One thing scans did not find was the space ship that escaped the station. It had to be somewhere, seeking some kind of repairs.

If they get on board again with the ambassadors, we'll have a real problem.

During the briefing, Fielding told them they were not to attack the ship if it tried to depart. Their allies in orbit would deal with that. If the marines were able to extract their packages, the bombers would come in and annihilate the facility. Heat was responsible for getting the people back to the shuttles and clear of the area.

I'm getting sick of these time crunches. Everything's a rush.

The shuttle broke the cloud coverage and the surface of the planet was revealed. He saw the facility nestled amongst gentle hills and grass. A forest sprawled off for miles in the north and the terrain became rocky on the east and west. Heat noted their landing zone, a clearing with a line of sight all around.

"Landing in two," Fielding announced. "Weapons up and at the ready. We'll be hauling ass the second those doors open."

Heat looked over his HUD, noting all systems were green. The others exchanged looks as the retro thrusters kicked in. The ship bucked wildly as it slowed to a halt, settling onto the ground. Doors dropped a moment later and the marines filed out in a rush, rounding the vessel and heading up toward the facility.

Two Pahxin shuttles landed on either side of them, massive transport class vessels. Dozens of men poured out, their bodies shimmering from personal shields. They wore black uniforms and carried short rifles with tiny scopes on top. Their forces would approach from the flanks while the heavily armored marines would go straight up the middle.

Heat double checked the new addition to his defenses, the short term personal shield the techs came up with while they were away on their last mission. They weren't sure how long it would last or exactly what it would defend against but he figured he'd kick it on before covering open ground.

One of the men joked about what would happen if the tech backfired. He speculated they might be disintegrated. His comments were enough to put some of the men off of even trying it. "We haven't needed it so far," Anderson said. "I figure they should test this crap better before they strap it on us."

"Don't you remember?" Gorman quipped. "We're the guinea pigs, man. If they need someone to try a weapon or piece of gear, they come to us. Besides, don't be an idiot. There's no way we'll be disintegrated. Blown up, maybe … but even so, the power core ain't big enough for a real explosion. So just relax. It might save your life."

At the end of the day, none of them had a clue what it would be like and their idle, paranoid speculation didn't do the technology any favors. For Heat's part, he intended to trust it. Harper hadn't done them wrong yet and he doubted her work would start just then.

Gorman hit the jump jets and Heat followed suit, rising above the hill so they could see over the walls. Several Tol'An troops were dashing into the courtyard to defy them, preparing their weapons. "We have contact," Gorman called over the com. "Forces are setting up a defensive position. Get ready."

"Be careful with explosives," Fielding said. "I'd rather we do some precision shooting until we know where the prisoners are and how we're going to get them out."

Beams tore through the air, two whizzing by Heat's head so close he should've felt the warmth from the attack. As he landed, he took cover behind a rock. A quick glance showed he could see over the wall. Targets had taken cover within buildings and against the walls of each structure. None of them were totally safe, not from the sheer numbers surrounding them.

Heat took aim and fired, catching his target in the chest. The man's shield might've saved his life but the concussion of the attack knocked him to the ground. Another took his place, firing wildly off to the left, toward one of the Pahxin units. Someone else blew him away, this time with a head shot.

Gore splattered the wall, proving the personal shield didn't extend to protect the skull.

Gruesome. I'll have to remember that.

Heat stumbled backwards as something hit his shoulder, a blast that didn't quite have the force required to punch through his armor. He dropped low and backed away, trying to see who made the attack. There was too much chaos to pick any one person out and he just kept up his own assault, firing at anything that moved.

The Pahxin blasted away at the area, covering the space with so much beam fire it was hard to see what was going on. Heat and the rest of the marines were able to advance, adding their own weapons to the mix. The Tol'An retaliated but they were unable to handle the overwhelming firepower.

As the joint attack continued, the Pahxin and Humans brought down dozens of Tol'An in moments. Private Kelly called out that he was hit in the arm, a blow solid enough to knock him to the ground. Heat dropped low and crawled over to check on him, but he appeared to be unscathed.

"How'd you pull that off?" Heat asked.

"The personal shield worked!" Kelly cried, crawling to his feet. He started firing into the compound again. "Gotta love that tech!"

Shouts from the left flank indicated the Pahxin weren't coming out completely unscathed but regardless, it became abundantly clear they would quickly secure the outside area. The Tol'An might have reinforcements waiting to engage but they'd have to come outside. When the enemy began to fall back, it looked like they definitely won.

"They're falling back!" Fielding shouted. "Cease fire and take cover!"

Heat wondered why he wouldn't have them press the attack but it occurred to him a moment later that the Tol'An might be trying to draw them into a trap. Not only that, but once they entered the base, the prisoners could have literally been anywhere inside and that meant friendly fire became a possibility.

The Pahxin also paused and Fielding went to confer with their commander. Heat had his men crouch, aiming at the opening. If anyone came out, they'd be done but until then, the marines would hold the area. It wouldn't be long before they'd be dashing inside to finish the foe off and get their people back.

The key now was to be patient, something Heat knew none of the marines were particularly good at.

☐
Chapter 9

Ulian's three ships moved in to engage the enemy ships and Desmond ordered the Gnosis to form up on their far left flank. He leaned forward in his seat, watching as they approached to conduct the attack. Fighters and bombers raced alongside them, ready to engage at a moment's notice.

Getting in so close to the planet allowed them to deploy the shuttles before the enemy had a chance to repel them. It made the operation considerably easier, at least at the beginning. A brawl between the larger ships shouldn't take too long, especially considering how powerful the Pahxin vessels proved to be.

Massive beams erupted from Ulian's lead ship, connecting with the scout. Shields burst in a moment and bits of the hull burst off in various directions. It returned fire, feebly turning to provide another angle to survive even a few more moments. Another shot caught them from a different Pahxin attacker, this blow enough to end them.

The scout went up so fast, they didn't even see an explosion. It was simply gone.

The rest won't be nearly that easy, Desmond thought. *Especially those big bastards. I guess we should be happy they didn't have an entire armada here.*

"Cassie," Vincent said, "can you detect any sign of the Orbs here?"

"No," Cassie replied. "Nothing on scans at least. If this is their main base and they're hiding them somewhere, they've found a way to mask their signatures ... which would be interesting considering. Once those things are on, the power emanating from them is intense."

"The Tol'An has more resources than this," Desmond said. "I guarantee it. Think about terrorist cells. They're difficult to take down because they spread out, put minor resources in many places. Even when there are competing factions doing the same thing, they have a hard time finishing each other off.

"When we take this out, they'll barely feel it." Desmond scowled. "Stopping them from this plan though ... that will be a blow they notice. Zach, target that destroyer and open fire."

"We're at long range, sir," Zach replied. "I'm getting a good lock now ..." He paused. "Opening fire."

The ship's deck vibrated in the familiar way as they unleashed on their opponent. It seemed to be focusing on the Pahxin ship but when the first blasts from the Gnosis caught it on the starboard side, it began turning in their direction.

"Looks like we got their attention," Vincent said.

"Damage?" Desmond asked.

"Minor to the shields," Salina replied. "Dropped to eighty-percent. There are fighters … No … they're larger than that … Perhaps bombers? Incoming now."

"Get our ships on them," Desmond said. "Take them out before they get in range. Keep on them, Zach. They're going to retaliate in a second and I'd like to have given them two volleys to their one."

The destroyer got their shots off first, strange blue beams that connected with the Gnosis bow and continued seamlessly for several seconds. Salina called something out but was interrupted by a deafening pop to the left. Desmond's ears rang and he noticed smoke coming from the wall.

As the beam dissipated, Salina shouted, "whatever that was knocked our shields out in the front! We've got a minor hull breach in the crew quarters that were merely damaged before but what's worse … our weapon systems are currently offline."

"Turn us!" Desmond called to Zach. "Show them a side we've got some defenses up. How long before weapon restoration?"

"I'm working with engineering now," Salina said. "I don't have an ETA yet."

"Get us one!" Desmond gestured to Vincent. "Make sure the bombers and fighters know we need some screening. Are shields even up on other parts of the ship?"

"Yes," Salina replied. "Just the bow is currently undefended. The other emitters are holding but I have to warn you, with the front down, the other generators are straining to compensate. I'm going to redirect power until we get that fixed. That will only take me a few moments. Engineering has just reported they are evaluating the problem now."

"Tell them they don't have much time," Desmond replied. He clenched his fist, considering the next course of action considering the situation. Falling back might be best. If they fired that weapon again, they'd simply tear through another part of their defenses. Still, such a thing must've drained considerable energy. "Cassie, what was that cannon?"

"I'm not sure," Cassie replied, "however, there was a massive energy surge when they fired it...enough so that they seem to have committed quite a bit to making the shot. I don't think they've got the power to do it again soon. We could be in luck. I'm guessing they hoped they would kill us in one go."

Vincent scoffed. "If they would've been patient and took some regular shots first, they might've."

The gravity of his comment wasn't lost on Desmond. "Inform the Pahxin vessels of what we just encountered. If those other ships have such weapons, they'll need to know. For now, give us some distance on this guy and let's see if we can't hold off on another round. Let the smaller ships handle some of the fighting."

***

Admiral Reach strained against the bonds holding him in place to a chair. He sat beside Raeka in an empty cell with metal walls. The door across from them slid to the left and they'd been led there by a couple of fiery soldiers who roughly dragged them down the hallway. Once inside, they were forced into the chairs and cuffed at the wrists then left alone.

Christina was wrong about the prisoner transfer. When the ship landed, it was inside the facility and ten armed guards arrived, aiming their weapons at the prisoners the entire time. They were led through the subterranean hangar and into a set of holding cells where they were deposited separately.

Not even ten minutes passed before Reach and Raeka were taken away, leaving Christina behind in her own cell. *I'm surprised they haven't killed her already. They only need us if they want to make a statement. Why hold on to the help?* The thought infuriated him but he couldn't help but feel pessimistic.

Several hours of waiting allowed misery to settle in. Reach's back hurt and his stomach growled. Thirst made his throat dry and his head swam. *Are these* bastards going to leave us in here to starve to death? What's their game? He turned to Raeka, clearing his throat to get the man's attention.

"Can you understand me?" Reach asked. "Hello?"

"I understand you," Raeka replied in a soft voice.

"Do you have any idea what they're doing? Why they're holding us like this?"

"The Tol'An wear their prisoners down," Raeka said. "We have not consumed in a long while and they will allow us to continue to suffer under these conditions. They believe it makes a man more pliant when questioned ... when pressed for information. We are to be interrogated, make no mistake but they will only do so when they believe we are prepared to talk."

"What could they possibly want from us?" Reach shook his head. "This makes no sense! Do they think they can get military secrets from us? Some kind of security clearance? What will they be after?"

"While I know their methods, their madness is beyond me." Raeka sighed. "It is impossible to say exactly what they will need but I can promise you only that it will not be pleasant. Even if we speak, I sincerely doubt they will treat us with the proper formalities of what prisoners should endure."

Reach was about to ask something else when the door opened and a man stepped in. He wore a black robe, the hood drawn low enough to obscure his face. He approached, standing silently in front of them for a good minute before turning his back on them. There again, he did not move and remained silent.

"What do you want?" Reach asked. "What is going on?"

"Ah," the Tol'An said. His command of the English language was disturbing. "You would like to speak. That is good. I am here to ensure you do. Shall we begin with introductions? My name is Gizan."

Raeka gasped. "Gizan Relik? But … it cannot be so! You were pronounced dead many years ago!"

"It is true, ambassador." Gizan said the word as if it were a curse. "And I have been living my life in defiance of what you have just described ever since. My master has changed but my purpose has not. I will bring order to the galaxy. The Tol'An will prevail and the two of you are in a position to help the cause."

"We cannot help you!" Raeka shouted. "Your kind, your people … They are nothing more than …" The rest of his statement devolved into Pahxin and Reach couldn't understand but he got the gist of it. It may have been profanity or just some particularly nasty comments but either way, it made Gizan take note.

The robed man spun in place and slapped Raeka across the face, halting his verbal onslaught. Blood coated the ambassador's pale cheek and he didn't

"That is quite enough out of you," Gizan said in a soft voice. "You should speak in the tongue this man understands. That way he might see what a monster you and your people are. In any event, we will now discuss a few key points about your facilities and how they are set up. I am particularly interested in how humanity defends technology."

"Well enough to drive you scum off," Reach replied, scowling up at the man. "Did you read the report about how we knocked out your little invasion force? Then hopped over and took the other Orb from under you?"

Gizan's eyes narrowed. "Yes, but we were not discussing effectiveness, were we?" He drew a knife from within his robes. "My master tasked me to bring you both back alive though he did not specify unharmed. Continue your defiance and you will meet him not entirely whole." His body seemed to tremble but a deep breath settled him. "Shall we try again?"

Reach met his gaze and shook his head. "Do your worst, you bastard. I'm not telling you a goddamn thing."

Gizan stepped in front of Raeka. "Do you share his sentiments? I believe he is a soldier while you're just a diplomat, a useless tool for the government. Will you accept pain to avoid answering questions?"

Reach examined his fellow prisoner and didn't like the look of him. His eyes darted about furtively, as if he might explode with anxiety. He strained at his bonds for a moment, hands clenching and loosening before his head dropped and his chin tapped his chest. Terror and physical discomfort must've gotten the better of him.

"What do you want to know?" Raeka asked. "You must understand, I am told little! Please, you know this! You used to work with us, Gizan!"

"Indeed." Gizan stepped forward and lifted Raeka's face, menacing him with the knife. The ambassador began screaming in his own tongue, struggling in vain as the blade slid over his ear. Blood flowed freely, covering his neck as his tormentor stepped back to give him some room.

Raeka gasped and moaned, his shoulders tensed up from the pain.

Gizan turned his attention back to Reach. "Do you see what I will do to my own people? They are like me…born of the same planet and species but you … you are little more than an animal. A back world germ allowed to cultivate too long. The things I am willing to do to you will be legend. Tell me what I want to know about your military force!"

Reach opened his mouth to offer up more defiance when an alarm went off overhead. Gizan's eyes widened and his head spun about like an animal cornered in its den. The expression made the admiral smile. "I seem to recall a similar situation for us not too long ago. You're not expecting company?"

"How?" Gizan shouted. "How did they find us!" He grabbed Raeka by the throat. "How! You will tell me now!"

The door opened and a soldier leaned in. Reach couldn't understand what he had to say but he rattled on and on for several moments. When finally he finished, Gizan backed away, aiming the knife at both men. "I will be back for you soon. Do not think you have been given a reprieve. This inconvenience only delays the inevitable. Believe me. You are both doomed."

And he left.

"What did the soldier say?" Reach asked. "What's going on?"

Raeka struggled to speak, trembling before he finally found his tongue. "He stated they had a problem ... that my people have arrived and deployed shuttles. The Tol'An were unable to muster their defenses in time to stop them but they are moving what vessels they have against our potential rescuers. Gizan was called away to guide the men here on the surface."

"How? How'd they find us?"

"Implanted ... tracker ..." Raeka coughed several times before continuing. "My people inject one into dignitaries when they do not trust the negotiations."

"Your government thought we might try to kidnap you?" Reach shook his head. "Thank God for paranoia."

"In this case, I will not apologize."

"Nor should you." Reach grinned and turned away, peering at the floor. *I'm sure you're out there with them, Desmond. There's no way you'd let them pull a rescue without the Gnosis. I need to find some patience and wait for the cavalry. Great timing ... There's no other way to say it.*

***

Cassie scanned the surface of the planet, surprised to find that there were no other sentient settlements. There were ruins, like other systems they visited, but no people. The Tol'An lived like rodents in the walls of an abandoned home, unnoticed and forgotten. She wondered how many other worlds they occupied in a similar fashion.

It must be plenty. The AIA has plenty of information on terrorist organizations. These guys are acting exactly the same.

She hoped to find Christina and the Admiral. Two humans among so many Pahxin shouldn't have been difficult. Unfortunately, their physiology proved too similar to differentiate between them in the compact facility. There were plenty of life forms but the specific ones she cared about were buried amongst them.

Scratch me helping the marines find the friendlies. I guess I'll focus on the dangerous ship blasting us with those insane weapons.

Thayne provided some feedback, letting her know that they must've used separate generators to power the weapon. None of the other Tol'An equipment showed an increase in their energy efficiency. Shields still operated roughly the same as the Pahxin vessels. That meant an independent source specifically for their new attacks.

Which also meant taxing their systems wouldn't necessarily take the weapon out. They could continue firing it long after the rest of the ship was disabled, even life support. Of course, that was contingent upon their power source remaining intact throughout combat. They needed to target it specifically.

Such a power source is likely to cause some serious damage if we take it out, too. Cassie thought. *Like a power core going up.*

She ran a scan over the destroyer, focusing on any energy buildups. As the weapon had to be recharging, she hypothesized that it would be somewhat obvious. Several key areas of the enemy vessel appeared on her screen and after a good twenty seconds, she started to get frustrated. *Maybe they have it shielded against this type of thing.*

But then she found it. A red blob in the middle of their hull, close to the power core itself. In fact, it seemed to be a second reactor on the ship. Further data came in, showing her that the strain from the weapon would've drained the ship completely, leaving nothing for any system aboard. If they hadn't installed the second source, the weapon would still be a theory.

Cassie related what she found to the captain.

"If we could take out the secondary reactor," Desmond said, "we'd be able to handle the first one and this wouldn't be a problem."

Vincent spoke up, "I can have the bombers give it a go. A couple bombs should take those shields down."

"I'm all for it," Desmond said, "but again, if we can do that, then we don't have to worry about the weapon. Taking the shields down will destroy the whole ship. One thing's for sure, the bombers will have a much easier time evading that thing. Unless Cassie has something to say about their targeting abilities?"

"No, sir," Cassie said. "Only how they power it."

"They're coming in again," Salina said. "Moving toward us."

"Vincent, redirect one of the bomber squadrons right away." Desmond gestured toward Zach. "I want full speed. Keep us out of their range and draw them back from the fight. With any luck, the Pahxin won't have to deal with them and can take out the rest of the force. We'll take the hard one, I guess."

A brief moment of pressure jostled Cassie in her seat as the ship picked up speed. She glanced at Salina's screen, swallowing hard at what she saw. The enemy was giving chase and they weren't slow. She didn't want to contemplate the stakes of the race they were getting into or the deadly implications of the rising meter representing the opponent's cannon.

***

Dennis Arden found himself back with his normal squadron, waiting for the chance to get into the action. Tol'An fighters had been deployed but they were brawling with the Pahxin, and dramatically outnumbered to boot. Raptor squadron went after the incoming bombers, Charger provided air support on the planet which left Mustang in reserve.

He wondered if Dala was out there as well. After her ship had been damaged, he figured she might be grounded but perhaps the Pahxin were able to carry plenty of spare. Their vessels were built for war, after all and though the Gnosis certainly came prepared, exploration always was the primary focus.

"Mustang One, this is Commander Bowman, do you copy?"

Dennis cleared his throat before replying. "I copy, what're our orders, sir?"

"I need your squadron to conduct some concentrated fire against the destroyer. Coordinate your attack runs with Rhino squadron. I'm sure you saw that weapon they fired at us."

"The beam," Dennis said. He watched it hit the Gnosis and was surprised when it lingered, continuing to cause damage until the shields visibly cracked. Luckily, Zach was able to get them turned so they couldn't get another shot off to the undefended portion of the vessel. "Do we know what it is?"

"We know it has a dedicated power source and they're charging it up," Vincent said. "We're also pretty sure they won't be able to target something so small as the fighters and bombers. That's why you're getting your shot on it."

"Won't this attract the attention of the enemy fighters?"

"Maybe, but we don't have a lot of choice. Besides, their smaller ships are pretty busy fighting with the Pahxin. You should have plenty of time to cause some trouble…even if it's just a distraction, we need some space to breathe if we hope to win that brawl."

"Understood. Rhino One, did you catch that?"

Nolan Coplan led the bomber squadron and he piped in. "Affirmative, but we're en route to the surface for our attack run. I'm sure we're not all needed for that. Do you want me to divide the forces to support Mustang?"

Vincent answered, "yes, make that happen and keep a tight report cadence. I want to provide frequent updates to the captain, especially as we're trying to contend with that weapon. Good luck, men."

Dennis drew a deep breath before engaging his thrusters. "I think you guys heard that," he said to the rest of his team. "Follow on my lead. Alicia, you especially. I want us coming at it from multiple angles to avoid their defenses as much as possible but be sure you're coordinating your shots. When the shields are weak, the bombers will hit them."

"Their shields should be way too much for us," Lieutenant Kate Zeller spoke up. "We need Raptor in here … maybe Charger."

"Charger's providing air support on the planet," Dennis said. "And Raptor's screening for the Gnosis. We've got a lot of firepower in six ships. Remember, we're trying to strain their power, not take it down completely."

Nolan added, "we'll time our bombs to make the most of draining their power too. You weaken them, we'll do the rest."

"There you go," Dennis replied. Scans came back, showing three sets of turrets on the bottom and top of the ship. They had good coverage but there was a small blind spot in the front, rear and sides. He tapped his computer, drawing out an attack vector for the other pilots that minimized their time in the path of the enemy's defenses. "Follow those directions and we should be golden."

***

Squadron Leader Dimitri Gerrit received a promotion to lead Raptor squadron after his predecessor died on their first mission. Since then, there weren't many opportunities to hone his command skills. He'd participated in their last mission but they were primarily backup, with only a little dogfighting.

This time out, they were in the thick of it back at the space station and his team was assigned to take on the bombers rapidly approaching the Gnosis. He took the lead, getting his people into a wide vanguard formation. The blips on their scans were large, roughly one and a half times the size of their own ships.

They had a good three minutes to kill before the enemies would be in range to shoot and Dimitri used the time to his advantage, trying to gather all the data he could on his targets. The computer suggested their maneuvering thrusters were not powerful enough to allow them flexible mobility but they had tough shields and thick armor.

It's going to take a few shots to bring them down.

Five bombers in total approached and six fighters raced to meet them. Time to target for the Tol'An was six minutes. Raptor had a tight window to finish them off before they could deploy their payloads and potentially destroy the Gnosis completely. Considering what the initial beam weapon did, the danger was very real.

The bombers housed defensive turrets and what the scans indicated might be countermeasures. This limited the use of missiles, at least initially. Depending on how they used their defenses, the bombers might not be able to fend off a large barrage. Dimitri's gut warned him that he had no idea what to expect from their opponents though.

Their countermeasures might scramble the friend or foe circuitry. Our own people have been working on a similar technology. Probably best to stick to beams and guns until we know more.

Flight Lieutenant Dylan Ball acted as his second. He'd also received a field promotion and proved to be a reliable member of the team. The two men maintained a private channel and it flashed on the HUD when they had less than ninety seconds before they could attack. Dimitri clicked over, letting out a sigh.

"Now's not really the time, is it? We're practically on top of them."

"I know," Dylan replied, "but I want to take two of the others and break from formation. We'll loop around and hit them from the flank. They don't seem all that maneuverable. We just have to coordinate it so we don't get caught up in friendly fire."

"Okay," Dimitri agreed. "Angle your attack. We'll be going head on and then climb. Relate it to the team and let's make it happen." He switched back to the open channel and Dylan gave them the plan. A moment later,

Raptor Two, four and six banked hard to the right and hit their afterburners, rocketing away.

We're the distraction, Dimitri thought. Gotta love being in charge.

The bombers began firing their turrets, total blind shots as if they were merely hoping for a hit. Dimitri forced himself to remain calm and fly steady. The chances of being hit at that range were negligible. Even if a stray shot found a mark, shields would absorb it. Only a missile would be cause for actual concern.

Lieutenant Marge Kingston, Raptor Three, spoke up on the com. "That's a lot of turret fire, sir. Recommend we dive and come at them from the bottom."

The bombers might be able to angle to continue shooting at them but the suggestion was still sound. It would put their opponents in a tough spot, especially with the other three ships on the verge of flanking them. We just have to buy another few moments. Dimitri approved the course change and the three ships dipped, dropping below the turret coverage.

"Go ahead and use your beam weapons," Dimitri said. "Let's throw some fire back their way and see how they like it." They had twenty seconds before they'd pass under the bombers. This changed the plan with the way they'd interact with their companions, only the fact they'd be diving instead of climbing.

Dimitri made the change clear to Dylan half a moment before pulling the trigger. Purple light cut through the darkness between them, splashing against the hardened defenses of the first bomber. *I can't believe I hit. I didn't even use my targeting computer.* The lucky shot had a positive effect as his opponent tried to climb, a reflexive twitch.

As the enemy altered course, he took himself away from his formation. His buddies must've had nerves of steel as they continued lumbering on as if they didn't even notice Raptor's presence.

Dimitri passed under the bombers in an instant, moving so swiftly the enemy was little more than a blur overhead. Dylan called their attack as he and his two fighters opened up, using beams and guns to lay into their targets.

If the enemy didn't care about Raptor before, they certainly did after that. Two of the five ships spun, giving their little squad more turret coverage. The one that broke formation took the majority of the hits from Dylan's attack run and Dimitri's computer showed that they waylaid the ship's shields, bringing it down below twenty percent.

As Dimitri's trio came around, they focused their fire on the straggler, tearing into him. In the ten seconds it would take to pass him by, they pounded him with a near constant state of beam weapons with a few shots from their guns thrown in. The bomber tried to maneuver away, spinning slowly as it dove but he just didn't have the maneuverability.

Sparks licked the hull and a moment later, it went up in a great plume of blue-gold light.

"Scratch one," Dimitri said. He turned his attention briefly to the scanner to see if any of the other targets experienced a significant amount of damage. That tiny distraction, that short moment his attention was diverted, something shook his ship, jarring him so hard his teeth chattered and his jaw ached.

Spinning to the right, Dimitri dove to avoid another blast from whatever hit him. Scans indicated one of the turrets caught him. Shields held at fifty percent. *Wow, those hit harder than I anticipated!* It dawned on him that their defensive weapons would have to be tough if they hoped to get close enough to deploy their ordnance.

I bet these are stolen military vessels. Dimitri clicked over to Dylan. "How bad did your pass hurt them? With one down, we've only got three and a half minutes before they can lob a bomb at the Gnosis."

"Two of them took a pretty nasty bump," Dylan said. "Only one came away completely unscathed and he's in the middle. Now that they've given themselves more coverage, he'll be tough to nudge out of there."

Marge butted in, "we can lob our missiles in and go for proximity charges. Detonate before they make contact."

"Good call." Dimitri looped around. "Fall in on me and we'll see what we can pull off. Dylan, you stick to guns and beams the rest of us will try Marge's plan."

The ships formed up loosely, giving themselves some space to maneuver in the event that more turret fire came their way. As they rapidly approached their targets, they found they'd easily overrun them if they weren't careful. Each ship launched two missiles, the heat coronas from the projectiles winking as they hurtled away.

Dylan performed a series of rapid shots, spraying the area in front of them with as wide a range as he could without altering course significantly. His attack was more about harassing their enemy, while giving the missiles a chance to arrive.

Two of the projectiles were taken down by turret fire but the other eight arrived unscathed. Dimitri gave the order to detonate and tiny explosions erupted around the bombers. The force of the blows caused the two on the ends to be shoved away from the center, dislodging them from their tight formation.

The unscathed ship dove, scans showing his shields took a bit of splash damage but he came away clean again. His companion didn't fare so well as two of the missiles blew right beside him. Shields dropped, shattering visibly with a burst of red sparks. "Focus on him!" Dimitri called, letting his computer grab a lock before firing.

Concentrated shots tore the bomber to shreds, leaving behind chunks of debris.

Flying Officer Carson Bright, Raptor Six, called an SOS, drawing Dimitri's attention. The young pilot took several blows from one of the turrets, knocking his shields out and bringing his engines offline. "I'm ejecting!" Carson shouted. "Ejecting!"

The life pod burst from his vessel and sailed off into space. Dylan broke formation and attacked the offending bomber. He took his target at the flank, banking just enough to avoid a series of shots from the defensive turret and hammering his opponent with guns.

Hull damage caused the bomber to spin to the left and the engines shut off. It might not have been destroyed but it seemed dead in space, drifting away from the action. That's three down. Dimitri thought. Two to go, including one that isn't even hurt.

The chronometer showed they had less than a minute to distract the bombers before they could attack the Gnosis. One was already on full defensive and trying to fend off the fighters so he wouldn't be a problem but the lucky one, the guy who hadn't even taken a direct hit, continued plodding along.

"Raptors three, four and five," Dimitri said, "you're on the harried one. Finish him off. Dylan and I are going to take the other guy before he gets any closer. We have to wrap this up, folks. Don't dally. A mistake right now means a lot more than some hurt feelings, believe me."

Dimitri directed his course, coming in behind his target. The ship's turret spun and started firing at him, causing him to drop lower to avoid the thing. Dylan came alongside him, dropping a few feet. This gave them a good angle on their target's engines and bottom, two sections which should have had the weakest shield presence.

"I want concentrated fire," Dimitri said. "It's the only way we're going to put this guy in the ground quickly enough to save the Gnosis."

"I'm ready," Dylan said. "Got lock. In three … two …"

Before they could get to one, the enemy bomber fired his payload, deploying six bombs in rapid succession. Dimitri pulled the trigger, unleashing hell on the ship and scored a direct hit. Dylan's attack helped whittle the enemy's defenses down and less than a few seconds later, they rendered him to burning embers.

"Shit!" Dimitri grunted. "Gnosis, this is Raptor One, we have a big problem. You have six bombs incoming. We are moving to intercept right now." He checked his scans and noted his people finished off the last of their targets. "Raptor, form up and help me take care of those projectiles. We've got even less time now so hurry! We're seriously at zero hour here."

Chapter 10

Christina leaned against the wall of her cell near the door, peering through the bars. They left her there alone, having taken the ambassador and admiral away a long time before. It gave her a chance to think in private, to examine the situation and figure out what to do next. The situation, dire as it seemed, had not taken all hope from her yet.

The Tol'An didn't bother with cameras, or if they did, they were well hidden. Their little prison was mostly crafted out of stone and concrete with metal bars and wooden planks for benches. There were no bathroom facilities in the area and they didn't bother to bring food or water.

Why bother to take care of people if you're just going to execute them. The thought made Christina scowl. Did the terrorists plan to kill them in some public way? Did they want to broadcast it back to the two governments as a way of establishing their credentials as complete psychopaths? She was pretty sure no one would've argued with them before this stunt.

Now we know for sure, I guess.

Christina wondered if they were trying to interrogate the other prisoners or merely torturing them. Either was a possibility but she didn't know what they could possibly be asking for. The Tol'An weren't about to invade anyone's space. They weren't going to Earth with an armada, at least not yet and the Pahxin seemed capable of repelling them on that front.

What was left? Did they want to find a way to infiltrate the society's through intrigue? That made some sense. But even so, what did they hope to achieve from Reach? All they needed to get into Earth's society was a safe place to land and a solid understanding of some language on the planet.

The Pahxin might even be easier to break into considering they used to be part of that society.

Ultimately, it doesn't matter what they want. We just have to get out of here. Christina considered her options. Escape would require a weapon and a method of getting off the planet as soon as possible. When they broke atmosphere and descended to the surface, she saw there was nothing for miles around.

Running for it would practically be suicide. If they didn't find a vehicle in the facility, leaving would be the same as waiting to be killed. No, she needed a ship and the only one she was certain of was the assault craft they were kidnapped on. I'm pretty sure I can fly it well enough to get off this rock but what then?

They saw defensive ships orbiting the planet. Getting away would entail weathering an assault by them, plotting a hyperspace course and initiating FTL all in short order. None of which she'd ever done before.

Christina understood the theory but putting it in practice under stress was a very different situation.

We have to try. Maybe the Pahxin ambassador can help.

Christina considered her next move and came up with something. It might be a long shot, depending on why they grabbed the ambassadors, but she figured there was no harm in trying. Dropping to her knees, she started shouting for help, putting on a show of misery and despair.

"Please! Just let me talk to someone! I'll tell them anything they want to know! I'm with the admiral all the time! Please ... I can't take the isolation anymore!"

Not the best performance, but it'll have to do. Christina kept it up, even going so far as to fake weeping. *At least the Tol'An don't know what true human misery is or they might see through this in a hurry.*

It took nearly five minutes of freaking out before one of the guards burst in and hurried over to her. He barked several strange words in her direction, speaking in his own language. Christina looked up at him through water eyes, shaking her head. "I'm sorry, I don't understand you ... I just ... I can help your boss ... I need to get out of this cell. I'll do anything!"

The Tol'An grunted and crouched in front of her, leaning close. She felt her muscles tense, prepared for action but she maintained her cool. Come on, put your face right next to the bars, buddy. You're so damn close!

"I'm ready to talk …" Christina tilted her head, holding his gaze with her eyes. He began to speak again and that's when she struck, lashing out to wrap her fingers around the back of his neck and yanking his face against the cool metal of the cage.

His mouth opened in shock and she drove the fingers of her free hand into his solar plexus. A gasp took him instead of a scream and drew back, hammering him once in the throat. He choked and started to collapse but she kept him close, rifling his pockets until she found the key. Next, she relieved him of his rifle and unlocked the door.

Christina stepped out of the cell and crouched beside the guard. She took hold of his head and wrenched to the left, straining until his neck snapped. Pocketing his keys, she searched the body and found a tablet. Grabbing that and his weapon, she hurried to the door open door.

She leaned to look out when an alarm went off, driving her back.

Are you serious? They must have cameras after all! Damn it! Christina aimed the gun and waited for the soldiers to come in but they didn't arrive. Instead, she heard people shouting and running away from her position. Maybe I'm wrong about what's going on. Finally, a little luck for a change.

Glancing outside, she saw soldiers rounding a corner, running away from her. They headed up a flight of stairs and disappeared. Shouts continued long after she couldn't see them. The muffled sounds of shuttle engines burst from outside followed by gunfire. A battle began and it was happening on the surface.

This might solve how we're going to get out of here, depending on who arrived. Christina drew a deep breath and departed the holding area, moving to the right toward the first corridor. Time to find the admiral and get out of here. I only hope the attackers out there are on our side.

***

Admiral Reach strained at his bonds, testing to see if he might be able to escape. Gunfire burst from above, muffled by the depths of the base but it was still quite apparent. He figured it would be better to attempt to meet their people rather than simply wait for them to arrive. If at all possible, getting away would help the rescue effort.

"There's no reason for that," Raeka said. "Stay still and be glad that we are rescued."

"I won't count on that until our soldiers are in this room," Reach said. Even then, he wasn't quite ready to give in to total optimism. He'd been involved in enough military operations to understand the risks inherent in them. Anything could happen, good or bad. Despite the overwhelming numbers, stray bullets didn't differentiate targets.

Gizan burst back into the room, eyes like a wild animal. He looked at the two of them, sneering. "I suppose it would be on you then," he said, pointing at Raeka. "It would be just like our government to put something in your body. I should have thought of it. I could've prevented this. I am truly a fool."

"This battle is over for you," Raeka replied. "Please … surrender, Gizan. Help us put an end to Tol'An aggression. Be one with your people again. This is your only option."

"I have many options left, filth." Gizan advanced and punched Raeka in the gut, making the man wheeze. "But the first of them will be to get the admiral here to my ship. Pity about you though. I do not have time to cut you open and find where the tracker is so you will simply have to die here and now."

Gizan drew the knife he'd used on Raeka earlier and drew it back, prepared to plunge it into the man's chest. Raeka cried out, shouting in his own language. Reach struggled so violently his wrists ached and began to bleed.

Just then the door burst open and Gizan stumbled back before he could land his blow. He spun, staring down the barrel of a Tol'An rifle held by Christina. "Sorry to interrupt," she said. "That looked like a pretty intimate moment. Would you mind stepping aside before I blow your damn head off?"

"Kill him!" Reach shouted. "Shoot this sick bastard!"

"No problem," Christina said. Her finger twitched as Gizan lashed out, knocking the weapon to the side. The weapon discharged, the beam splashing harmlessly into the wall.

Gizan followed up with another blow to the weapon and Christina lost her grip, blocking another blow meant for her face. He stabbed at her with the knife but she caught him by the wrist, slamming her knee into his gut. A grunt of pain racked his throat and he stumbled back, giving them both a chance to square off.

Christina lifted her hands defensively, stepping to the left until she stood between Gizan and the prisoners. He lowered his center of gravity, holding his hands out to either side. She threw a feint to the left and he bought it, lifting his arm to block. Before he could recover, she kicked him in the gut, driving him back against the wall.

Before Gizan could move, Christina hopped forward and pummeled his face and chest with a series of swift punches. He tried to slash her with the knife and cut her shirt just below the ribs.

Gizan overcommitted to the attack and half spun in the effort. Christina booted his elbow, disarming him of the knife, then followed up with another kick to the back. The blow knocked him to the floor and he scrambled away, climbing to his feet with a savage snarl.

Christina backed away, as if to give herself some space to size up the situation. Gizan jumped at her, grabbing her about the waist and lifting her off the ground. She clasped her hands and slammed them down on his back three times before they hit the wall. His grip loosened and she shoved him away.

A punch to his face made him scream and he returned the blow, catching her on the cheek. This time, Christina dropped to the floor and she rolled over on her back.

"Come on, Major!" Reach shouted. "Don't let this Tol'An trash take you!"

Christina scooted away as Gizan advanced. He wrung his hands into fists as he approached, smiling wickedly. "I will eat your heart, human. Devour your very essence and leave you to rot here on this miserable world. You have failed."

Gizan lunged forward and Christina bent her knees, catching him with her feet. Shouting with the effort, she shoved him away and he stumbled backward into the wall. Reclaiming her feet, Christina advanced and kicked him in the groin then followed up with another blow to his face. Gizan lurched away and grabbed the door before slipping through.

"Did he just run?" Reach shouted. "That bastard is fleeing!"

"I'm not going after him," Christina said, grabbing the rifle from the ground. She aimed at the door as she moved close to the chairs, drawing a set of keys out. "Let's see if one of these will unlock those cuffs."

Reach struggled a bit as he impatiently waited for her to free him. "Good work, by the way. I can't believe you escaped."

"I told you it just required some patience." Christina paused as one of the keys worked. She handed them to him. "Please free yourself the rest of the way, I'm going to guard the door until we're ready to get out of here."

"Do you know what's going on out there?" Reach asked, scrambling to get the other binding off.

"I came immediately to find you, so no." Christina manned the door and peered out. "Whatever happened it gave us the chance to get out of here though so I'm not going to look it in the mouth."

"Good plan." Reach stood and moved over to Raeka. "Come on, pal. I'm not leaving without you."

"Thank you …" Raeka nearly sobbed as the bonds came free. "Both of you, thank you."

They joined Christina at the door. "We're ready to move."

"Okay …" Christina hummed. "I'm trying to decide the best course of action. I'm not in the mood for friendly fire, that's for sure."

Reach noted that her face was swelling up and she was bleeding from the knife cut to the chest. "Are you going to be okay, Major?"

"Believe it or not, I've had worse times." Christina offered a grin. "Follow me, gentlemen. I'll do my best to get us out of here. Let's just hope whoever came along isn't particularly trigger happy. This will be a real short escape attempt if so."

***

Desmond stood as the destroyer closed the distance between them. The Gnosis was moving at full speed and still the enemy was gaining on them. Zach fired but they didn't even try to avoid the attacks, instead soaking them with their defenses as they moved in for what would undoubtedly be the kill.

"Their weapon seems to be powered up," Cassie said. "It's ready to fire again."

"Remember," Salina said, "they get two shots with their weapon before it has to recharge. We cannot take them head on. The shields are too low and the generators can't handle it. Advise we show them our aft."

"Do it," Desmond said. "Hurry, Zach. Redirect all weapon power to the engines. Buy us distance and give the fighters time to do their work."

"Report from Raptor," Vincent sighed. "It's not good. The bombers were able to deploy a payload on us. Our people are trying to shoot them down before they get here."

"Great ... Will our turrets be able to help with those bombs?"

"I'm on it," Salina said. "I'm going to have to leave them some power though. They'd be part of redirecting from weapons."

"Keep them online and do whatever's necessary to protect us against those bombs."

Zach got them spun so that the destroyer was looking at their rear. The weapon fired again, cutting through their shields as before. The attack splashed on one of the engines, making the entire ship rattle violently. The ship lurched and they seemed to stop. An eerie silence fell over the bridge before all systems kicked back on.

"Report!" Desmond called. "What happened?"

"One of our engines is offline," Salina said. "Shields are down."

"I've got no maneuverability," Zach added. "Helm seems to be offline."

Vincent turned to his console and spoke harshly into the microphone, giving the pilots an update on their situation. He made it clear that the pilots were responsible for keeping them alive. The notion might've been a lot of pressure but he was ultimately right. If they weren't able to harass that destroyer or take out those bombs, the Gnosis was done for.

The next few minutes and a bunch of fighters stood between them and oblivion.

***

Gizan made his way from the holding cell and down the hall. The fight with the human did not go at all as he intended. He had no idea they could be so formidable or well trained. Especially a woman. Why would they bother to give them such education? He underestimated her and paid the price for it.

I am lucky to be alive. The shame would rest on him for some time but he did not have time to wallow in his failure. He needed to escape the facility before the Pahxin and human forces took it over completely and he was captured. His incarceration or execution would be a huge blow to the Tol'An.

Several soldiers huddled near the stairs leading to the entrance. He stopped when he realized they were without a commander. "What are you men doing down here?" There must've been over two dozen of them, perhaps more. They were crammed into the rooms and corridors, looking uncertain and afraid.

"We are unsure of how to proceed." One in the front said. "The enemy has surrounded the base."

"Then drive them back!" Gizan shouted. "Get up there and slaughter every one of them to the man! This is our facility and you will not allow it to fall to filth! Go! Bring glory to the Tol'An!"

The speech wasn't exactly his most rousing but it had the desired effect. He lit a fire under them and the men charged up the stairs, their guns leading the way. Any moment, they would enter another firefight and this time, it would distract the enemy long enough for Gizan to slip away.

I hope they repaired the ship enough for my departure. Gizan ran down the hall toward the underground hangar. He not only had to contend with departing the planet but he needed to set a course that would get him well away from the forces surrounding the system. *They will likely be too busy with our defenders to give chase.*

Two men waited near his ship as he emerged and they stood at attention when he arrived. "Get aboard," he ordered. "We must flee here immediately and tell the master what happened. This facility is lost but we may still have victory if our lives are preserved."

They powered up the engines and started off through the cave that would take them out of the area and some miles from the base. By the time their enemies knew where they went, they'd be long gone. A quick trip to orbit then we will hop to the next system and finally home. I will have much to answer for but not to these bastards.

Gizan leaned back in his seat and glared out the cockpit as they headed toward the bright, sunlit exit. He drew a deep breath and prepared himself for the trials to come. *The master may judge me. Only him. All the rest will simply forget my name ... which is all the better for the Tol'An cause.*

***

Dennis watched the timer on his HUD countdown backward from six. The destroyer just unleashed fury upon the Gnosis and seemed to cause considerable damage to the engines. Mustang squadron needed to up their attack and drive the destroyer back if they wanted to have a home to return to.

The timer hit zero. He pulled the trigger, his energy beams striking the enemy shield the same time as several others. Scans showed the shields were definitely weakened, especially since the target chose to take the direct hit from the Gnosis. They would have two full volleys before having to reposition for another run.

Their target's shields needed to drop down to at least sixty percent to make the bomber run worthwhile. Anything greater might be little more than a nuisance.

Turret fire tried to dissuade them, and one shot came close enough to Dennis to sizzle his shields. Still, they had found an ideal space to fly in, allowing them to avoid the majority of the defensive blasts. A second timer went down, this time from three. At zero, Dennis was only a thousand kilometers away.

He fired again and pulled up, banking away from the enemy and hitting his afterburners.

"Nolan," Dennis spoke into the com, "are we good? What're the shields at?"

"I hate to tell you this," Nolan replied, "you're going to have to make another run. You only got them down to seventy-eight percent. It's climbing back but if you're quick, you should have it."

Dennis sighed. "We're on it. You heard him, guys. Line up for a second attack run on my mark."

He set the timer even faster than before, a countdown from three for the first attack. The others formed up and they sped toward the destroyer, through considerable turret fire since they didn't have the chance to line up their attack as carefully. The timer hit zero and Dennis fired, his blasts striking the shields again.

On his second attack, he let loose two missiles at the very end and climbed. As the projectiles found their mark, he was nearly two thousand kilometers away, just out of range from the turrets.

"Damn it," Shane said. "I got tagged back there pretty bad. Shields are down in the rear."

"Are you still maneuverable?" Dennis asked.

"Yeah, but I can't take another one of those."

"If we have to go back in," Alicia spoke up, "I can hit it a few times. I can make it out of there."

"Shouldn't be necessary," Dennis said through gritted teeth. "Nolan, please tell me you guys are able to get in there now."

"They're at fifty-eight percent this time," Nolan replied. "We're deploying bombs now!" Twelve bombs in total were fired and they rocketed forward two at a time. Each successive hit would batter the moderately weakened shields and hopefully, take them down significantly enough to end the fight.

Dennis glanced over his shoulder to witness the first two hit. They crashed against the shields and lit up brightly, turning the entire area white. Before the light even faded, the next two hit and the next. By the third couple projectiles, orange flames joined the white. The Destroyer turned but it was too late to avoid the damage.

The enemy ship didn't explode but it was no longer chasing the Gnosis. As it drifted off, sparks erupted around the damaged hull. The rest of the bombs found their mark, further amplifying the destruction. Pieces of the vessel cracked off and were launched into deep space. Scans showed the ship's power was currently disabled.

"Mustang One to Gnosis," Dennis called out. "Do you read? The destroyer seems to be down."

"Good job," Vincent said. "Fall back and do what you can to assist Raptor squadron. They're chasing down some bombs that are incoming. We're not out of this yet."

Just when I thought we'd have a chance to relax for a second. "Roger that, Gnosis. We're en route." Dennis adjusted course and gunned the throttle. "You know what this means, folks. Frying pans ... fires ... We have to find a way to keep ourselves out of both and still get home alive. Throttle up and move out."

***

Heat stared intently at the door, itching to get into the base and find their VIPs. The lieutenant was hanging around near the Pahxin commander, talking it out. Maybe they had a way of scanning the area to get a layout but it didn't feel like they had time. Somewhere in that place was a spaceship and that meant another way out.

They could be flanking us right now for all we know. Heat looked at Gorman. "What do you think?"

"I think we're sitting on our asses when we should be pounding dirt."

Heat brought Fielding up on his com. "Sir, permission to—"

Before he could finish his statement, a group of screaming men burst forth from the doorway into the facility. They began firing as soon as they stepped outside, firing wildly in all directions. Some took cover and others charged as if they didn't care what happened to them but even the computer was having a hard time putting their numbers on the screen.

Christ! Heat dropped lower to use the wall for better cover and fired his weapon, taking shots at anyone he could connect with. His HUD flashed a warning as an explosive flew by his head. A grenade landed less than five feet behind them. "Hop!" He shouted. "Frag! Go! Go! Go!"

The marines hit their jump packs just as the grenade went off. The concussion of the attack caught Heat from behind and sent him hurtling into the ground in the midst of several of the enemies. They opened up on him just as he initiated his personal shield. The first two shots were absorbed but the others struck his armor, causing the HUD to go red with a warning.

He hit the thrusters again but they didn't work. Dashing forward, he put his shoulder in front of him and slammed into the nearest soldier. The man was lifted off the ground and carried until Heat slammed into a wall, busting through the concrete into the room itself. This bought him some cover.

His shoulders ached and a point in his back had a sharp pain. The armor indicated there were some serious points of damage and the power assistance threatened to seize up. He kept his weapon aimed on the hole he'd made and backed into the corner so he could watch the door. Gorman's voice echoed in his helmet and he finally had a chance to acknowledge it.

"I'm alive, but I'm not sure how long I can count on that," Heat replied. "Armor got seriously hosed in that attack. You okay?"

"We're fine … Stay put. We're coming to get you."

A man burst in through the door and took a shot, narrowly missing Heat's head and connecting with his shoulder instead. Heat returned fire, catching the target in the stomach and face, spraying blood everywhere. He crouched, waiting for another attack which came almost instantly.

Firing again, he killed three more before he knew he needed to get out of that position. *If they come at me through the door and the hole, I'm done. I can't defend it with my armor in this state anyway.*

"I've gotta get out of here, guys," Heat said. "If you're coming, you need to hurry. Otherwise, I'm going through that hole and taking my chances."

"You're an impatient ass," Gorman said. "I'm at the door to the house now. We're locking the perimeter."

Heat moved over to the hole in the wall and peaked out. The Pahxin had engaged and were storming the facility. Gunfire filled the air, mostly energy blasts that seemed to sizzle as they passed by. More than once, he was nearly caught in the face and he pulled back just as something connected with the wall beside him, sending chunks of debris over him.

Another shot caught Heat in the left arm and he spun into the room, taking cover again. "It's insane out there!"

"That's why we're securing the perimeter," Gorman said. "Hang tight and keep your head down. Something stirred these guys up and they're not playing around anymore."

Heat listened to the fighting, waiting for it to subside but it wasn't slowing down. His HUD showed there were still plenty of enemy targets out there and they were really pushing hard. Several Pahxin suffered in the attack and the com traffic indicated they were nursing quite a few wounded.

His armor indicated he'd been hit too, a crack to the side of his back that was going to take some work from the doctor. The hit he took to the left shoulder might've dislocated it but it had already gone numb so he didn't notice. As he took stock of his situation, he heard a noise from the other room.

"Friendlies incoming!" Gorman shouted. "Do not fire, Heat! I swear to God, I'll smack you!"

"It's about damn time," Heat replied. "How're we doing this?"

"The Pahxin are almost done." Gorman turned and fired. "We need to get into the facility. Can you move?"

"Well enough." Heat didn't genuinely believe it but he wasn't going to sit back while the others went without him. "Lead the way."

Heat followed Gorman through the door into a space with no walls and a partially caved in ceiling. He didn't remember hearing any explosives go off but that was the only way the place could've been so devastated. Outside, four of their marines held the area, rapid firing in every direction.

Tol'An bodies littered the area and the moment Heat stepped outside, Gorman waved his arm for everyone to follow him. They dashed for the facility, blasting their way through a small squad of six before they arrived at the door and headed down a flight of stairs. Vine's personal shield took a hit but kept him safe.

Those things aren't useless after all. Wish they worked a little longer. I wouldn't be so messed up.

Gorman held up his arm for them to stop and he paced into the hallway, aiming his weapon. "Who goes there?" He shouted. "You're coming on some highly armed marines so if you can understand me, you'd better speak up!"

"Hold your fire," a woman's voice called back. "This is Major Dawson. I've got the ambassador and admiral with me now!"

"Any more guys down here?" Gorman asked.

"Not that we saw on our way out. Do you have a way out of here?"

"Soon as we mop up the forces up there, we sure do." Gorman turned to Heat. "I guess we found our VIPs."

"Seems they were more capable than we thought," Heat replied. "We have to get them back to the shuttle. Now that we know where they are, we can get some air support in here and strafe those bastards."

"Gorman to Fielding, we have the VIPs and are ready to come out. What is the situation, over?"

Gunfire turned sporadic and they heard only a few shots as opposed to the constant barrage of a few moments before. It lasted another twenty seconds before the lieutenant responded. "Enemy has ceased fire. We need to clear the area, get to the evac and let the bombers finish this place off. Come on out."

"We're clear," Gorman said to the others. Major Dawson, Admiral Reach and the Pahxin ambassador approached.

"Glad to see you, boys," Reach said. "I didn't know if you'd make it but I had a feeling Captain Bradford wouldn't let us down."

"Glad to be here, sir," Heat said, gesturing for them to come forward. He scanned them for injuries and noted that the ambassador required medical attention but the others were only a little battered. They'd be fine. He spoke into his com, "we're going to need medical personnel standing by when we return to the ship."

"Everyone okay?" Gorman asked.

Heat nodded. "We need to get out of here."

"Wait!" Christina stepped forward. "If you've secured the area, we can't go without grabbing some intel. This place could be a gold mine."

"We're about to level it with bombers," Gorman said. "We don't really have time."

"Call them off," Christina replied, turning to Reach. "Sir, surely you agree. We have to find a computer terminal at the very least and see what we can pull. This sad tablet I grabbed won't offer much insight."

Reach seemed to think about it for several moments before nodding. "Alright, the major is right. Let's get what we can from this place. There's no reason to waste an opportunity like this. Tell he bombers to hold off. This shouldn't take long."

Heat held back an urge to sigh and turned away, reaching out to Fielding. "Lieutenant, the VIPs are secure. I need you to let the bombers know we require another few minutes. The admiral would like to gather some intel from this facility before we depart. Please advise."

"Sounds good," Fielding came back. "We've secured the courtyard so you should have a few minutes but don't take long. We have no idea how long it will be before the Tol'An send reinforcements."

"Understood." Heat drew a breath and gestured down the hall. "I'll escort you while we make this happen. Gorman, take the Pahxin ambassador up to his people for some aid. This shouldn't take long."

☐
Chapter 11

Dimitri figured the bombs wouldn't be all that difficult to destroy. The challenge came from their speed but they moved in a straight line, driving toward their destination. With any luck, when one exploded, it would take others with it. He figured the bomber only deployed the payload out of desperation.

Lining up with the heat corona of his target, Dimitri engaged the targeting computer. It failed to get tone immediately, which surprised him. He was at medium range and there was no reason it should've been a struggle to lock on.

"Are any of you having trouble with your computers?" Dimitri asked. "I can't seem to get tone."

"Same," Dylan replied. "There's some kind of field surrounding them. Looks like we have to eyeball the shots."

Dimitri engaged a reticle, lifting his nose to lead the target a little. He fired and the beams seemed to be on target. The bomb climbed at the last second, avoiding the attack. Are you kidding!? "Did you see that?"

"Let's escalate things," Dylan said. His ship pulled away from the others, moving closer to the projectiles. He opened up with guns. The shots hammered one of the bombs, even as it also attempted an evasive maneuver. A bright spot near the engine lit up and the casing shattered, sending debris in all directions. "That's one … but holy crap, they're quick!"

"If they detonate, we can't be so close to them," Marge added. "I'm going after them from the flank. Maybe I can strafe them and do some real damage."

She banked to the left and headed off and Raptor Four, Jerry Graff, followed.

Dimitri climbed, noting they had less than four minutes before the bombs reached their target. Five remained and if all of them were allowed to hit, they would certainly cause enough damage to destroy the ship. After the most recent attack by the destroyer, the Gnosis was in no shape to take additional shots.

"Need a hand?" Dennis Arden tapped into their com channel. "Looks like you're having some challenges taking down some bombs."

"They've got evasive capabilities," Dimitri said, firing his weapons. Again, the bomb danced away but he continued after it, chasing the thing as if he were in a dogfight with it. "Do you see this?"

"We can help," Dennis replied. "If we lay down enough concentrated fire, that should be sufficient to take them out. We're coming in hot. Watch your scans."

"I've got an idea," Flying Officer Alicia Quinn piped in. "Permission to break formation?"

"Granted," Dennis replied. "But keep it within some realm of safety, huh?"

Dimitri knew Alicia well enough but he didn't know she was such a daredevil. After their last couple missions, her name became a byword for reckless but daring flying. If she had a plan, he could definitely assume it would be wild but whether it proved effective or not remained to be seen.

Another of the bombs went up as Marge caught it on the side with guns, tearing through the fuselage and knocking it out.

Maybe they're not responding to the guns the way they do the beam weapons. That would make some sense and give us a slight advantage. Dimitri relayed his epiphany to the others. "Try to switch to mass drivers as your primary attack. Let's see if they don't bother to evade."

"Hold on," Alicia said. "Don't shoot at all for a second. I'm trying my plan."

With four left, Alicia flew in front of the bombs, firing her beam weapons at the one on the end. It climbed and she spun in place, firing again. It tried to evade and collided with another bomb, detonating when they made contact. The resulting explosion took both out and Alicia righted herself, climbing to rejoin the others. "Two left."

"That was ridiculous." Dimitri muttered, firing his cannons. The bomb didn't move nearly as much as it had when they used beam weapons but he still narrowly missed. "Everyone, just lay into them together!"

They had less than a minute left. The Gnosis loomed head of them, easily large enough to block out the distance beyond it. Every fighter, eleven in all, fired their cannons at the same time, laying down a wide field of fire. The bombs wriggled and tried to evade but there was simply too much ordnance for them to avoid.

They were torn apart, tumbling away. Dimitri slumped in his chair, feeling a sense of relief wash over him.

"Watch it!" Dennis shouted. "I'm reading unstable mass ... The warhead's intact!"

Dimitri climbed suddenly, pulling up hard and hitting the thrusters. An explosion behind him made the ship shake violently and he struggled to maintain control. Thrusters on all sides kicked in, forcing the ship to remain straight. Alerts burst in his ears, crying out that the engines had taken significant damage.

"Everyone okay?" Dimitri called. "Did anyone get caught in that blast?"

Each Raptor and Mustang sounded off but two reported heavy damage. They needed to get back aboard the Gnosis to have their problems looked at but as Dimitri looked over the hull of their home, he realized they might be in more trouble than he anticipated. The damage looked extensive and potentially crippling.

Dear God ... Can we recover from all that? Time to find out.

"Return to base, everyone," Dimitri said. "Our part in this fight is over."

***

Desmond gazed at the screen, giving his crew some time to catch up on the emergency repairs. The two remaining Pahxin ships brawled with the larger Tol'An vessels, blasting away with beams easily the size of some of the medium ships in the Earth defense fleet. As the enemy retaliated, the scene inspired awe, especially with the eerie silence of the chaos.

And we're sitting ducks all the way out here. Desmond sighed. I want to get in there.

Scans indicated there was tremendous amounts of debris in the makeshift battlefield, turning that area of space into a hazard for regular travel. Pahxin fighters overwhelmed the Tol'An resistance as tiny flashes provided some sense of the wild dogfighting. The battle seemed on the verge of conclusion but it wasn't over quite yet.

One of the two Tol'An capital ships took three shots straight to the hull. Their shields must've dropped and when the attack took them, electricity and fire poured out of several holes. Each engine produced a blue glow and the middle of the vessel expanded then burst, essentially cutting the ship in half.

The other turned, engaging engines while attempting to flee. They were immediately pursued and the Pahxin concentrated their fire, chipping away at what remained of the target's defenses. It couldn't stand up under the barrage and the thrusters went dark a moment later as it began to drift.

Desmond's com chimed and he tapped the screen to bring it on speaker. "Go ahead."

"Captain, it's Webber. I've finished the damage assessment. Of the two primary engines, only one of them will require repair. As a result, I've restored the helm so we should be able to move again."

"How fast can you get the engine back online?" Desmond asked. He wondered how long they'd be stuck in that system, especially since the place was hostile territory. The Tol'An might respond when they lost connection to their outpost and if the Gnosis remained in a weakened state, they wouldn't be able to defend themselves.

"Half an hour at most ... That's just to get us moving again. When we get home, we'll be busy for a while." Webber sighed. "Shield generators were burned out so we're replacing the circuitry. They're internals are all modular, meaning it won't take long. We've almost got them back up. Some of the emitters will also have to be replaced. A couple melted completely."

"Understood." Desmond smirked before he asked his next question. "What about weapons? Hyperdrive?"

"Surprisingly, our arms are still ready to go. If you need them, you've got them." Webber spoke to someone else for a moment before returning. "Hyperdrive remained unscathed. Sorry, something's requiring my immediate attention. I'll report back with some progress ASAP. Webber out."

Desmond turned to Salina. "How are our casualties?"

"Eight dead so far," Salina replied. "Many wounded but I'm receiving reports that the med bay has stabilized the worst of the injuries."

"Vincent, are we getting any word back from the pilots?"

"Most of them have returned to base," Vincent replied. "The bombers have just finished leveling the facility. The marines are on their way back. They report they have the admiral and his aide. The Pahxin ambassador has gone back with his people. Com chatter suggests that the Tol'An have been routed and are fleeing the battle ... though I have no idea where they're going."

"Ulian has hailed us," Salina said.

"Put him on the screen." Desmond stood when the commander's face appeared. "I understand you've taken care of your side of the battle."

"We have. I would like to commend you on handling that destroyer. The technology aboard, so I'm told, was something we had not seen before. Very powerful. Good work. I am sorry that your ship received such damage from it. We would like to send a repair crew to assist with preparing you for hyperspace."

"Thank you, we accept." Desmond clasped his hands behind his back. "You seemed to make out fairly well."

Ulian waved his hand. "Conventional weapons. They did not have the advantages of your foe. Nevertheless, yes, they were tough but not insurmountable. I will leave two ships here to mop up and come to you personally for the assistance. Stand by."

The screen went dark and Desmond sat back down, fending off the stress that settled on the back of his neck. They may have succeeded at their task but the cost was high. Several crew dead, equipment damaged...it was the worst battering they suffered since beginning their forays into space.

I suppose we'd been fairly lucky until now. I underestimated the Tol'An before but I shouldn't have. The Pahxin would've wiped them out by now if they weren't formidable. It won't happen again.

"Captain," Salina said, "I'm picking up a large ship leaving the planet's surface. It's not one of ours." She paused. "It's the one that left the station! I'm sure of it!"

Desmond scowled. "Where's it going?"

"I ..." Salina stopped suddenly. "It's coming this way!"

"Are the shields back?" Vincent asked. "Or at least some of them?"

"Yes, sir," Zach answered. "I've brought them online for the starboard and aft sides."

Desmond nodded. "Turn us so he has to face the defended side and get the weapons ready. If he's really going to attack us, we can give this bastard a special thank you for leading us here."

"Um," Cassie said, "permission to put something on screen?"

"Go ahead," Desmond replied.

Cassie tapped at her computer for a moment and a tactical view of the area came up. "I did a scan on that incoming ship. They're powering up their hyperdrive but that looks like an attack run to me."

Desmond watched the screen for a moment and sure enough, the ship was coming straight for them.

Perhaps they planned to offer up a parting shot before dashing away. I wonder if we can disable that arrogant ass before he escapes. "Zach, lock weapons on target and fire a full volley."

"Yes, sir." Zach performed a quick set of swipes on his console. The lights dimmed low when he fired but came back quickly enough. He switched the screen to straight visual. "Direct hit!"

The enemy's shields brightened even as it launched a projectile and veered away. It seemed to have maneuverability more akin to a fighter than they would've expected given the size. Smoke bloused out from the top of it just a moment before it winked into hyperspace and disappeared.

"Damn it!" Desmond clenched his fist. "I can't believe he pulled that off. What's that projectile it deployed?"

"Some kind of missile ..." Zach frowned. "The warhead seems ... Wow, suggest we pull away as quickly as possible."

"Are the shuttles back on board yet?" Desmond asked. "Everyone from the surface?"

"Negative," Vincent said. "The admiral's ship has yet to take off and his fighter cover is still above the planet's surface. The bombers haven't finished off the facility yet either."

"What're they waiting for?" Desmond shook his head. "It doesn't matter. Get us away from that thing and target it. We're not taking more proximity damage from these guys."

The ship lurched as Zach engaged the engines and they pulled away, slow at first but the speed picked up. Ulian came on the screen, face contorted in concern. "What has happened? I did not expect you to move."

Desmond filled him in on what was happening and had Salina send the scan data about the missile. The readings made the Pahxin commander frown and he turned away, shouting in his own language. When he finally looked back at the camera, he straightened his shoulders before speaking again.

"We have seen this type of tactic with the Tol'An before. Those weapons are deadly to smaller ships and can cripple larger ones. While the destructive power is nothing to sneer at, they produce a field which disables computer systems. Those include life support."

"What do we do about it?" Desmond asked.

"Do not shoot it." Ulian's eyes narrowed. "Do you have tractor beams?"

Desmond shook his head. The concept was known to them and their scientists were working on prototypes but they had yet to be implemented. Grabbing something with energy sounded useful but ultimately, it wasn't the thing to focus on while trying to go beyond the borders of their solar system.

"I'm afraid not."

"Then we will be there soon. We can contain the explosion with ours …" Ulian paused, as if considering his words carefully. "You will still want to continue moving away from the attack though. Just in case."

"You heard him, Zach," Desmond said. "Give us as much speed as you can muster. Oh look…Webber's calling with a complaint about this, I'm sure." He brought the engineer on the line. "I don't have time at the moment. I'll get back to you soon. We're … essentially racing for our lives up here."

"Understood … just …" Webber grunted. "Try to take it easy? A little?"

"No promises." Desmond clicked off the com and sat back in his chair. He turned to his own computer, checking the proximity between the Pahxin ship and theirs. The ETA was less than a minute but it felt like an eternity. The missile kept pace with them, even gaining slightly. An estimate showed it would hit them in less than two and a half minutes.

Sweat broke on his brow. *This is far closer than I'd like to admit.* He felt the tension on the bridge. Every one of them understood the danger barreling down on them, the helplessness of fleeing. One more brush with death, another threat with heavy ramifications. Once they left the Gaeliran space station, they found themselves hounded by misfortune.

"Twenty seconds to impact," Zach said. "I've got her at full speed but it's not enough!"

Desmond gripped his seat as the Pahxin ship approached. A red, translucent beam burst from their bow, nearly hitting the Gnosis. Desmond turned to his computer and noted they caught it less than three hundred yards from impact. His eyes widened for just a moment before he regained his command cool.

"Keep moving, Zach," Desmond spoke softly. "Give us a little more room."

That was way too close. He thought as the missile detonated harmlessly within the tractor beam. Which pretty much sums up this entire mission. "Thank you, Ulian," Desmond spoke without turning on the com. "Slow us down, Zach and let Webber have some time to fix the ship up. I think we've had enough excitement for this shift."

"Admiral's ship is finally taking off," Vincent said. "They gathered intel from the facility and the bombers are about to take care of the rest."

"Sounds good." Desmond rubbed his eyes. "Salina, coordinate with the Pahxin to get some repair crews over here. I'd like us to be hyperspace ready by the end of this shift if at all possible. The longer we linger here, the better chance we'll meet up with more Tol'An, especially since one of them escaped. I think you all have something to do so let's move out."

☐
Epilogue

Christina sat in the shuttle, willing her muscles to relax as they lumbered back to the Gnosis. Admiral Reach seemed to be asleep, leaning his head against the metal panel of the wall. She needed to speak with him, not only about what they encountered but her allegiance to the AIA.

ETA to the ship showed twenty more minutes so if she wanted relative privacy, she needed to talk right away. The marines were busy talking amongst themselves and they were far enough away that if Christina kept her voice down, they wouldn't hear. Might as well get this over with before we have an audience.

She nudged him with her elbow and he started awake, glaring at her. "Are we almost there?"

"Yeah," Christina replied, "about twenty minutes out. I'd like to talk to you about events on the station ... and who I work for."

Reach lifted his brows. "Yes? You want to talk about the fact the AIA planted an agent with my staff?"

Christina nodded. "I'm hoping we can keep this on the down-low. It won't do anyone any good to bring it to light. I can retire from the position ... make it a clean but discreet break."

Reach sighed, turning away. "I'm not sure that suits me. If Dulain owes me a favor for example ..." He paused. "However, there is the matter that you risked your life for us ... multiple times. You could've played the role of an aide to the end. There's something to be said about that."

"What're you thinking then?"

"Maybe there's a good reason for you to stick close."

Christina narrowed her eyes. "I won't be able to tell you anything about AIA activities."

Reach shrugged. "No ... but I think we could reveal what happened here to Dulain and maybe work together instead of ... whatever this was about. I suggest we talk to him and see what we can do."

Christina looked out the window and sighed. Dulain would not be particularly pleased but considering the situation, she didn't have much of a choice. Maybe she shouldn't have told him who she was, it simply proved the fastest way to get him to listen to her back on the station.

I'm paying for it now. "Okay," Christina agreed. "We'll talk to him. But please ... don't tell Captain Bradford. We'll keep this to ourselves, deal?"

"Indeed, Major." Reach smirked. "And you can tell me more about how you got this rank ... and who you really are ... later."

"Yes, sir." Christina sat back in her seat, her muscles just as tense as when she tried to calm down minutes before. "Thank you for your discretion."

"And thank you for everything you did." Reach gripped her arm tightly, meeting her gaze as she turned to him. "You very likely saved my life. I won't forget it ... believe me."

Christina finally smiled. In the end, despite the factions playing against one another and everything that happened, they were two human beings who managed to survive the worst possible conditions. While her infiltration of his inner circle may have been discovered, she would have rather had to deal with that than the chance he could've died on the station.

***

Desmond wanted to meet Admiral Reach in the hangar as soon as he returned but duty kept him busy. They weren't able to hook up until two hours later, after the Pahxin repair crews were in place to help Webber prep the Gnosis for the return trip home. He had Cassie meet with them ahead of time to look over the intel they got from the station.

He figured putting an AIA agent on the task would be the best bet and she got Thayne involved right away. Her report was interesting enough that he planned to bring some of it up in his quick conversation. While the Tol'An base they found was not a large one, it did provide them with the coordinates to several military targets.

Desmond went to the admiral's quarters and knocked, entering when summoned. The older man sat on the bed, dressed in loose fitting trousers and a white shirt.

"Forgive my appearance," Reach said. "The doctors assigned me to some bed rest for the trip home. It was an order I didn't feel up to arguing about."

"I understand." Desmond nodded. "I'm glad to see you alive and unscathed."

"Thanks for coming for me." Reach leaned forward. "I had no doubts … but thank you. That madman … He would've murdered us. If not in that base, then wherever he planned to take us."

"Good Lord." Desmond clenched his fist. "I'm glad we got here in time. The intel you brought back paid off. We located several other bolt holes the Tol'An set up shop. We've even got the coordinates for a manufacturing plant where they've been producing their weapons."

"Do we know where they're keeping the Orbs?"

Desmond frowned. "I'm afraid not. We're guessing that's their main base. It's unlikely any of these smaller bases will lead there. And unfortunately, we weren't able to take any prisoners. One ship escaped … The one they took you out on from the station."

"Then the man who was interrogating us must've survived." Reach cursed. "I had some hope…maybe his own people will take care of him for failing."

"It's possible," Desmond said. "They're a special kind of crazy."

"Ship looked pretty damaged on our approach." Reach stood up and stretched. "Will we be able to get home?"

"Yes, the Pahxin helped with the repairs and they've certified the hyperdrive. You'll have plenty of time to rest before we get back too."

"Good. Before that, I have to speak with their ambassador." Reach turned to the desk and clicked on his tablet. "Is there anything else you'd like to talk about?"

"No, sir. I'm good. Just wanted to check in and let you know how we're doing."

Reach clapped him on the shoulder. "I'm glad to be back and believe me, if anyone doubts what you guys are doing out here ... If the council decides to be critical, I'll be there for you. I've got your back, Desmond. Thank you. For everything you've done on this mission ... thank you."

"Of course." Desmond smiled. "I'm just glad you're okay. We'll talk again before we get back. Until then, good luck with the ambassador though after what you guys went through together, I doubt you'll need it."

Printed in Great Britain
by Amazon